THE ROYAL RABBITS

ILLUSTRATED BY
KATE HINDLEY

THE GREAT DIAMOND CHASE

SANTA MONTEFIORE

SIMON SEBAG MONTEFIORE

First published in Great Britain in 2018 by Simon & Schuster UK Ltd
This edition published in 2020

Text copyright © 2018 Simon Sebag Montefiore and Santa Montefiore
Illustrations copyright © 2018 Kate Hindley

1 3 5 7 9 10 8 6 4 2

Simon & Schuster UK Ltd
1st Floor,
222 Gray's Inn Road
London WC1X 8HB

www.simonandschuster.co.uk
www.simonandschuster.com.au
www.simonandschuster.co.in

Simon & Schuster Australia, Sydney
Simon & Schuster India, New Delhi

A CIP catalogue record for this book is available
from the British Library.

PB ISBN 978-1-4711-9462-7
eBook ISBN 978-1-4711-7148-2

This book is a work of fiction. Names, characters, places
and incidents are either the product of the author's imagination or
are used fictitiously. Any resemblance to actual people living
or dead, events or locales is entirely coincidental.

Printed and bound by CPI Group (UK) Ltd, Croydon, CR0 4YY

To Tara

PALACE GARDENS

THE SHARD

THE WEEPING WILLOW AT GREEN PARK

THE RIVER THAMES.

BUCKINGHAM PALACE

ROYAL RABBIT H.Q.

THE RABBIT KINGDOM

buck male rabbit

bunkin country rabbit

bunny young rabbit

doe female rabbit

Hopster large, strong and clever rabbit

Thumper Special Forces
commando rabbit

CHAPTER ONE

An alarm screamed and lights flashed! Footmen ran and maids squawked! Royal corgis barked and police in black hurried to the scene! Blue lights flickered . . .

Buckingham Palace was in uproar!

But Shylo Tawny-Tail, the smallest of the Royal Rabbits, who was meant to be protecting the palace, was asleep on duty. He heard the faint sound of alarms and shouts in his dream, but didn't stir. Shylo had made himself a snuggly cocoon up in the velvety pelmet of one of the royal curtains which had made a perfect hammock, and was having a lovely dream about a weak and feeble country bunny who had helped save the Queen of England from a vicious plot by the fearsome Ratzis. As a reward, that small bunny had been invited to join the Royal Rabbits of London, a secret society devoted to protecting the Royal Family and fighting evil across the world.

Shylo had eaten far too much at lunch - how could he say no to a third helping when cabbage was one of his favourite foods? - and with a belly full of delicious cabbage he'd become very sleepy indeed. So, even though he had only meant to close his eyes for a moment, he had been napping for most of his guard duty . . .

Now, stirred by all the rumpus, the little rabbit slowly began to wake up. 'Turn that horrible alarm off,'

he grumbled as the noise made his sensitive ears ache.
Then he sat bolt upright and peered down from the
curtain with his one good eye (the other, remember,
was covered by a red eyepatch to correct his squint).
Shylo's stomach cramped with panic as he watched
the manic activity going on through the double doors
at the opposite end of the state room. He realized
something big had happened.

From his hiding place in the pelmet, he could see
the King and Queen being escorted by police officers

into the Diamond Room on the other side of the corridor. Now you may already know that the Crown Jewels are kept under guard at the Tower of London - *everyone* does! What you may not know is that the Siberian Diamond, being so very valuable, is kept in a special room in the palace, near the Queen's private apartments.

Shylo gasped in dismay. *Oh no*, he thought, ears flopping over his forehead. *Not the diamond . . .*

Realizing it was his duty to investigate, he jumped from one pelmet to the next. He paused a moment as more panicking footmen and Secret Service agents ran past, then he slid down the curtain to the floor and hopped across the crimson carpet to hide behind the door frame. He looked across the corridor into the Diamond Room where the full horror of the drama was unfolding.

The King was scowling; the Queen was frowning;

police officers were gravely shaking their heads; the Private Secretary, Sir Marmaduke Scantum, was wringing his hands; Lady Araminta Fortescue, the Queen's lady-in-waiting, was pointing . . . Shylo looked in the direction of her finger and finally saw what the commotion was all about. A display case stood surrounded by shattered glass; a small cushion in the centre lay empty . . . the Siberian Diamond was GONE!

Shylo blinked. Surely he was still dreaming. He *hoped* to the Great Rabbit in the sky that he was and he pinched himself just to make sure.

Ooooh! That hurt!

He wasn't dreaming. Someone had crept in and stolen the famous Siberian Diamond and he had been asleep the whole time . . .

The Siberian Diamond, dear reader, was not just any diamond, it was the biggest, most beautiful one in the

whole world, and the Queen's favourite jewel. However, it wasn't her favourite because of its size or value, but because of something far more extraordinary. You see, the gem was flawed, which meant it had many lines and waves and scratches inside, and when people stared into it they might see mountains, or rivers, or ships on the sea in the imperfections, the same way that you can make shapes out of clouds.

What no one knew, not even the Royal Rabbits, was that every time the Queen looked into the diamond, which she did whenever she felt a little weary, she would see a simple cottage, in the middle of a wood, and herself in the garden there, clipping the roses and enjoying the bees like an ordinary woman living an ordinary life. The sight soothed her and made her feel happy, momentarily taking her away from the often tiring life of duty and service (being Queen is not only about riding in a carriage and wearing a crown).

Once a year, on the first of May, the Queen allowed the Siberian Diamond to be taken to the Tower of London and put on display for one week only. Thousands of people queued up just to admire the beautiful jewel in its bullet-proof glass case, which, supposedly, made it impossible to steal. It was kept in a similar case at the palace, and was thought to be safe, but even unsinkable ships sometimes sink, and now Shylo realized that unstealable diamonds could be stolen too.

He watched with sadness as the Queen started to weep and the King went to comfort her. Shylo's ears drooped with guilt, his heart filling with shame that he had been sleeping while this outrageous robbery had taken place. It was all his fault. How he wished he could turn back the clock! He was so overcome that he didn't hear the growling of the Pack, the Queen's corgis, who had spotted the little rabbit and were slowly sneaking up on him. The Pack liked nothing more than fat, juicy rabbits, but even a scrawny, bony rabbit like Shylo was worth chasing.

Suddenly, Shylo got a whiff of dog - not only did he have sensitive ears, but (luckily) a highly sensitive nose as well. He looked down the corridor and spotted the fearsome corgis advancing.

He glanced around quickly, trying to work out an escape route. The hidden entrance to the secret network of tunnels beneath the palace was on the other side of the corridor, which was both wide and exposed. But what choice did he have? He could scamper back up into the pelmet because the dogs wouldn't be able to climb the curtain after him, but this was no time to hide: he had to return to The Grand Burrow at once and inform the Royal Rabbits of the robbery.

Shylo glanced back at the weeping Queen. The

sorry sight gave him a rapid surge of courage, like a fire in his belly (where the cabbages had been). He held his breath and dashed into the corridor. The Pack were now very close indeed and he froze in terror for a moment at the sight of the ferocious dogs. Messalina, their yellowed-fanged leader, curled her lip and growled. Then she quickened her pace. With his heart in his mouth, Shylo darted across the carpet towards the potted plant that concealed the secret tunnel entrance.

The dogs were almost upon him. He could feel their breath on his fur. With a shaky paw, he reached behind the plant and pushed a hidden panel in the skirting board. The door opened and Shylo fell into the tunnel with relief. He shut the panel behind him just as Messalina's wet nose thrust itself into the gap, then withdrew with a yelp.

Shylo jumped on to a chute and slid all the way

down into The Grand Burrow, which was the home of the Royal Rabbits of London, and his home now. He was safe, albeit a little bit shaken.

CHAPTER TWO

'Where have you been?' asked Generalissimo Nelson calmly as Shylo burst into the war room, out of breath and in a terrible panic. The little bunkin looked down the big table at the four large Hopster rabbits staring grimly back at him, and one ear flopped over his eyepatch because he felt so ashamed that he had fallen asleep on his watch and therefore been unaware of the terrible crime that had been committed.

'While you've been gone, the Siberian Diamond has

been stolen,' said Laser, the American Jack Rabbit, slapping her whip on to her leather boots in agitation. 'How do we know that? Not because the Royal Rabbit on duty informed us, but because we heard the alarm bells all the way down here in The Grand Burrow and looked through the periscopes to see police all over the place, and everyone gathered in the Diamond Room!' She looked at him and narrowed her blue eyes. 'So, where were you, Shylo, when you should have been watching the palace?'

Shylo didn't know what to say. He shuffled and the other ear flopped over his good eye. He made a great effort to lift it, otherwise he wouldn't have been able to see at all.

'Well? Answer the question!' boomed Zeno in his Jamaican accent as he flexed his huge muscles. Shylo began to tremble. Zeno was the Marshal of the Thumpers, the elite fighting force of the Royal Rabbits, and the huge Hopster was five times the size of little Shylo and extremely fierce.

Shylo's bottom lip began to tremble.

'That diamond is so large I often used it as a mirror,' said the elegant, grey-haired Clooney who was lounging in a chair, stroking his whiskers and looking dashing in his tuxedo. 'With its many surfaces, I was reflected a dozen times!' He turned to the little rabbit. 'So, where *were* you, Shylo? It was stolen on your watch.'

'Well?' asked the Generalissimo, arching an eyebrow.

Shylo gulped. He didn't want to admit that he'd been asleep on duty. He *couldn't* admit that. He'd only just been invited to join the Royal Rabbits - how could he tell them that he had failed, that the stolen jewel was all his fault? Luckily, his fur hid his blushes as he looked from one Royal Rabbit to another.

Just then, a soft voice broke the silence. *'Oh là là!*

The most beautiful diamond in the world is LOST?'

They all turned to see Belle de Paw sashay into the room. Her fur was rich and amber-coloured and she wore a flouncy lilac dress accessorized with little jewels pilfered from the Queen's bedroom. ('She has so many, what is one less!' Belle de Paw always sang in her musical French accent.) She strode up to the table in glittery high heels and waved a paw in the air. 'Why do you think Shylo is here? To inform us of the robbery, of course! Let us focus our minds on important things, like finding the missing diamond!'

Shylo gave her a grateful smile and her brown eyes twinkled at him warmly.

The Royal Rabbits turned away from the little bunkin and looked at Nelson. Shylo was very relieved.

'This is no ordinary diamond,' Nelson murred gravely. 'It's the legendary Siberian Diamond. Tell us about it, Clooney.'

Clooney got up from his chair and hopped across the room, admiring his reflection as he passed a mirror. 'Gosh, I am so handsome,' he whispered as he straightened his bow tie. He positioned himself behind a tripod where a projector had been set up to beam pictures on to a white screen. The other Royal Rabbits gathered round and Shylo followed sheepishly behind them, struggling with his guilt - he wished there was a hole in the ground which he could dive into.

Clooney clicked a button on a remote and a photograph of the Siberian Diamond appeared on the screen. Even though they had seen it many times, everyone gasped in awe: it was the biggest, brightest, shiniest diamond they had ever seen. No one gasped louder or with more longing than Belle de Paw, however. She loved diamonds more than anything.

Belle put a paw to her mouth and sighed. *'Oh là là! It is truly magnifique!'* Suddenly, all the diamonds she

had stashed away in her burrow seemed small and dull by comparison.

Clooney cleared his throat. 'The Siberian Diamond was found one hundred and thirty-two years ago by a Russian peasant on the snowy tundra of Siberia. He was grooming his old horse when he noticed a strange lump in the nag's dung. Thinking his horse had digested a potato and desperate for a good meal, the man delved enthusiastically into the pile of poo and pulled the object out. He was very disappointed when he discovered that it wasn't a potato, but something hard, sharp and inedible. Once cleaned, it became clear that it was an enormous diamond and most likely very valuable. Hoping for a reward, the peasant gave it to the governor, who was very patriotic.

'"This diamond belongs to the Empress," the governor announced, and, after wrapping it in a velvet cloth, he sent it on a sleigh all the way to Catherine the Great in her palace in St Petersburg. Catherine said it was so bright that she could read by its light.

'It remained in the Winter Palace, the official residence of the Russian Tsars, until just over one hundred years later, when legend has it that the Tsar lost it in a bet to his cousin, the King of England. But no one knows for sure. Somehow the diamond ended up in Britain and the Russians have wanted it back ever since. The British say it's unsporting not to honour a bet and have always insisted it belongs here. The Russians, of course, disagree.'

'So who took it?' asked Laser.

Shylo hopped closer to the screen, dazzled by the picture of the mesmerizing diamond.

'Well, that's easy,' replied Zeno confidently. 'The Russians of course!'

'*Oui,*' murred Belle de Paw, staring at its brilliance. 'If I had lost a diamond of that size, I would most certainly want it back.'

'But why would they wait a hundred years to steal it?' asked Laser.

'They've repeatedly asked for it back, but their request has always been denied,' Clooney told her. 'Perhaps they just got fed up with asking and decided to take matters into their own hands.'

'It's probably on its way to the Kremlin right now!' said Belle de Paw.

'The Kremlin?' asked Shylo.

'It's where the President of Russia lives in a fortress with red walls and pointed towers,' Clooney informed him.

Shylo prayed to the Great Rabbit in the sky that the diamond hadn't already been taken to Russia. He'd never forgive himself if the Queen's favourite jewel was gone forever, all because he had fallen asleep on duty.

'I'm not so sure,' said Nelson, banging his stick

with its silver rabbit head on the floor. 'The Russians are certainly likely suspects, on the grounds that it belonged to them in the first place and they feel it should be returned to them. But I hesitate to throw blame without having any hard evidence to go on.'

Belle de Paw narrowed her brown eyes. 'Imagine how popular the President would be with his people if he returned the Siberian Diamond to Russia. After all, it is the greatest diamond in the world,' she murred.

'Whoever stole it won't have left the country yet, unless they acted very quickly. I suspect the diamond is still in London,' said Nelson calmly. 'And, if it is, we're going to get it back. Clooney, Laser, Shylo, go to Number Ten Downing Street at once,' he commanded. 'See what intelligence ST-BT has for us. Belle de Paw, to the periscopes. I want to know everything that's going on in the palace. Zeno, prepare your Thumpers for a fight. If we discover the Russians are behind this, well, you know what *that* means . . .' And he looked grimly at the Hopsters who looked grimly back at him.

Shylo frowned. The other Royal Rabbits knew something about the Russians that he didn't. Something terrible. What could it be? The little bunkin felt a shudder run down his body. It started at the tip of his left ear and rippled all the way down to his right hind paw. He had been on many adventures since leaving his country home: outwitting the Pack of snarling corgis, escaping from the clutches of the evil Ratzis and even overcoming his fear of foxes in the Fox Club beneath Number Ten Downing Street. He hadn't imagined there was much else to be afraid of. But he sensed that another adventure was about to begin and he was going to need to summon his bravery once again . . .

CHAPTER THREE

A little later, Shylo sat in a big leather armchair next to Clooney and Laser. All around, bushy-tailed, sleek foxes played poker at green velvet tables, snookered balls on the billiard table, danced to jazz music blaring out of the jukebox and sat at the bar, drinking Butterscotch on the Rocks.

The taint of fox was overpowering, but Shylo was used to it now, because this buzzing place was the Fox Club, right underneath Ten Downing Street, and home to the foxes who worked alongside the Royal

Rabbits and looked after the Prime Minister. Once Shylo had been afraid of these fearsome predators, but now the bushiest and glossiest of all the foxes was sitting opposite him and Shylo wasn't at all frightened.

His name was ST-BT, which was short for Sharp-Tooth-Bushy-Tail, and, in all of London, there was no more splendid example of a fox. He had rings on his paws, dazzling white teeth, a gold chain around his neck with letters that spelled out STBT just in case anyone forgot who he was (which they never did) and, as usual, he was utterly calm.

Clooney had started to tell ST-BT about the robbery, but, of course, the fox already knew about the missing diamond. He made it his business to know everything that went on at Number Ten Downing Street - as the Prime Minister had learned about the unfortunate incident, so had ST-BT.

'We live in dangerous times, rabbits,' he said in his rich voice. 'But, before we get down to business, join me in a little drink. Three Butterscotches on the Rocks?'

'Yes, please!' replied Shylo eagerly. (One of the best things about visiting Downing Street was the yummy drink that gave him a warm feeling in his belly!) Clooney and Laser enjoyed butterscotch too and nodded at the fox.

'Coming up,' said ST-BT, waving his brush at the bar-vixen in a silver tuxedo and matching shorts. She began to mix the cocktails in a shiny silver shaker, engraved, of course, with the initials ST-BT, like everything else in the Fox Club.

Once the drinks were served, the three Royal Rabbits listened eagerly to what the fox had to say.

'The palace informed the Prime Minister of the robbery a short while ago,' said ST-BT, sipping his butterscotch through a silver straw, without making the slightest noise. Shylo tried to copy the fox, but made a loud slurping sound, which was very embarrassing. Ignoring the little rabbit, ST-BT steepled his paws and knitted his eyebrows. 'A missing diamond is a very delicate matter, to be sure.'

His voice was so deep and rich it was *foxifluous*. It would have struck fear in a small rabbit's heart had Shylo not known any better. The little bunkin's hind paws dangled off the edge of the armchair because he was so small, but ST-BT looked at him in the same way that he looked at Clooney and Laser, as if he, too, was a Hopster rabbit, not a bunkin from the countryside, recently made a Royal Rabbit.

'You need to hop carefully, my friends,' ST-BT added darkly.

'What does the Prime Minister think?' asked Shylo eagerly, because he wanted so very badly to get the diamond back for the Queen - and for himself, so that he could stop feeling guilty. 'Does he think it's the Russians?'

Clooney cleared his throat. 'What Shylo means to ask,' he murred smoothly, looking a little irritated by Shylo's sudden outburst, 'is whether the Prime Minister has any idea who could have stolen the diamond.'

ST-BT swished his brush. 'Oh, he doesn't know anything,' he replied with a chuckle. 'Without me, he'd be in a real mess. But, at the moment, Britain is good friends with Russia. We don't want to spoil that–'

'But the diamond means so much to the Queen. I

saw her cry,' murred Shylo, his heart slumping once again as he thought of Her Majesty's sorrow, which was all his fault.

ST-BT gave a chuckle that sounded like gold nuggets rattling in a pan, but he wasn't smiling. In fact, he was looking rather scary. 'Like I said, these are dangerous times and you need to hop carefully.'

'If the Russians *did* steal the diamond,' said Laser, 'they're insulting not just the Prime Minister but you, the Fox of Power!'

'But my friends, you don't have proof,' ST-BT growled. 'It's much too easy to blame the Russians because the diamond once belonged to them. That doesn't mean they stooped so low as to steal it.'

'Perhaps we don't have proof,' agreed Clooney, 'but *you* must know more than you're letting on. Come on, ST-BT, you know everything. Surely you have more information!'

How clever Clooney is, thought Shylo, *using flattery to get answers from the fox.*

'True.' ST-BT stretched lazily and swished his tail. 'All right, Clooney. I do know something and it *is* a little concerning.'

Shylo and the others leaned forward to catch ST-BT's words.

'Yesterday my agents spotted something worrying at the Russian Embassy in Kensington.'

'What?' asked Shylo, ears standing up with interest.

'Minks.'

This time even Clooney seemed shocked. 'God help us!' he groaned.

'Jeez!' muttered Laser. 'Minks? How many?'

'Ten or so. Enough to worry about,' ST-BT replied. 'And these aren't just any minks. Our secret agents say they're the Kremlin's finest. Highly trained little killers with the softest fur and the sharpest teeth.'

'It would be just like a mink to sneak into the palace and steal that diamond,' said Clooney.

Before Shylo could ask what minks were, a flash of red moved swiftly through the club, like a streak of fire. It stopped beside ST-BT's chair and Shylo saw it was Red Velvet, one of ST-BT's top agents. She was fit and elegant in a crimson tracksuit. 'I have news,' she announced and she gave her gloriously bushy tail a swish.

'Ah, Red Velvet,' said ST-BT. 'Do share it! We're among friends.'

The vixen looked very serious. Whatever information she had it wasn't going to be good. 'A big Mink-Boss has arrived in town,' she said.

ST-BT's top lip curled as he grimaced, revealing a long white and exceedingly sharp tooth. Shylo watched the fox's eyes narrow so that they became slits which glinted like blades, and his body stiffened,

as if he was preparing to pounce. This was not very encouraging. If ST-BT was concerned, they should *all* be worried.

'A Mink-Boss,' ST-BT repeated. 'One of the Kremlin's dreaded assassins-in-chief.'

At the mention of the Kremlin, Shylo felt a stirring inside his belly, which told him that something wasn't quite right. It was a little niggle, like he sometimes got when he was about to tuck into a big, juicy cabbage but sensed there might be a worm inside. The niggle was usually right (and had in the past saved him from eating many a worm), but he hoped very much that this time he was wrong. (It was quite hard to tell the difference between hunger and a niggle, and it had been a long time since lunch.)

ST-BT looked at the Royal Rabbits and nodded slowly. 'If a big Mink-Boss is in town, something's up.'

'Something big,' said Laser.

'To collect the Siberian Diamond perhaps?' Clooney added.

'Maybe,' ST-BT agreed with a shrug, glancing at his agent. 'Red Velvet, watch the minks' every move – where they go, what they do, even what they eat. I want to know every detail, understood?'

'Got it, boss,' replied Red Velvet, and with that she swished out of the club, leaving nothing but a flash of red and the taint of fox.

ST-BT looked at each Royal Rabbit in turn. 'Let's not jump to any conclusions. I always like to see hard evidence before I leap into action. The minks might be here for an entirely different reason.'

'All right, so we need to find proof that the minks have the diamond,' said Laser, pushing up off her chair. 'And we need to move fast, before they spirit it away to Russia!'

Shylo got up too and put a paw on his belly. There

it was again, that niggle. He wondered what it meant. But there was no time to think about it now. They had to get back to The Grand Burrow at once and inform Nelson about the minks.

CHAPTER FOUR

Shylo, Laser and Clooney climbed into the little underground railway cart which sped them back to The Grand Burrow along tunnels deep under the streets of London. As they rattled along the tracks, Laser and Clooney were quiet, alarmed that Russian minks were loose in their beloved, peaceful London. Shylo's tummy was rumbling now and, although he tried hard to focus on the minks and the missing diamond, he couldn't stop himself wondering what was for supper.

HOW DO YOU SPOT A MINK OF THE KREMLIN?

Minks of the Kremlin are a secret service of killers who live in luxury beneath the Grand Kremlin Palace and have worked for the rulers of Russia for a thousand years. If the rulers of Russia don't like someone, these minks pay them a visit.

Minks are cousins of the weasel. They have long, silky bodies, short legs, small heads, tiny ears and snub noses. They are very quick and have sharp little teeth.

Minks of the Kremlin are mostly covered in rich brown fur which is so deliciously soft that sometimes you might even forget about their teeth. They can be black or, very occasionally, white.

Minks of the Kremlin have white patches above their top lips: they look like they have white moustaches.

Minks of the Kremlin are experts in all the martial arts and always wear white judo pyjamas.

Minks of the Kremlin are very cunning and clever and can be vicious which is why they make perfect assassins.

The greatest enemy of the mink is the fox. Minks are very nervous of foxes.

Minks of the Kremlin speak Russian. They say *nyet* for no and *da* for yes.

Minks of the Kremlin eat fish, fish eggs and meat, but they'll tuck into just about anything as long as it's not past its sell-by date. (They are incredibly fussy about sell-by dates.)

Minks of the Kremlin are very clean and like to wash themselves a lot. They love water.

And now a special operations group of minks was in London . . .

At dawn the following day, Nelson and the Hopsters gathered in the war room, looking at a map of the Russian Embassy in Kensington Palace Gardens (which is also known as Millionaires' Row because so many rich people live there).

'How many minks?' Nelson asked.

'At least ten,' Laser replied.

'Ten minks are no match for my Thumpers!' boomed Zeno, flexing his big muscles.

'Ten minks are enough to secure the diamond and guard it on its way out of London,' Clooney added.

Just then, Shylo's tummy groaned so loudly that they all turned and looked at him in surprise.

'Haven't you had breakfast?' asked Nelson.

'I don't think it's a hunger growl,' said Shylo. 'It's a niggle.'

'A niggle?' Nelson repeated.

'Yes, a niggle. It's a feeling that something's not right.'

'Aha, an intuitive niggle,' murred Nelson, understanding at once. 'A sense of foreboding.'

'He's talking RUBBISH!' boomed Zeno impatiently, turning back to the map. 'Otherwise he would have got a niggle the day the diamond was stolen.'

Shylo's ears flopped over his face and he lowered his eyes regretfully. 'Niggles don't always come when you want them to,' he murred in a quiet voice.

'We've no time to listen to your niggles,' exclaimed Zeno.

'Not so fast,' Nelson murred, raising a shaky paw. 'Go on, Shylo.'

Shylo managed to lift one ear, but the other remained drooped over his eyepatch because everyone in the room was now looking at him, which made him rather self-conscious. 'I just keep thinking that it seems obvious that the Russians want the Siberian Diamond enough to steal it, but is it too obvious?' he began. 'I think my niggle is telling me that there's something else going on.' Shylo took a breath, shrinking slightly beneath the weight of so many eyes. 'What if the person who really stole the diamond wants us to think it's the Russians, but it isn't them at all?'

'Shylo is right,' murred Belle de Paw. 'It could be a very clever plot to fool us into chasing the wrong creatures!'

Clooney stroked a whisker. 'I'm not so sure,' he said. 'If it's not the Russians, who else could it be?'

'ST-BT told us that Britain and Russia are friends now so maybe someone wants to ruin that?' Shylo murred, trying to sound confident, when inside he felt very small and foolish.

'The only creatures who'd want to create that sort of mayhem are the Ratzis and they're not clever enough to sneak into Buckingham Palace and steal the diamond,' argued Laser.

'I agree,' said Clooney. 'But the minks are clever enough to get through the defences.'

'Which is why it must be the Russians who stole the diamond!' Zeno boomed. 'And we need to find out where they are and send in the Thumpers to get it back. We have no time to lose!'

Shylo could see that only Belle de Paw believed him and he began to doubt himself. What if he was wrong after all? Perhaps he wanted to get the diamond back too badly, because the robbery was all his fault and he felt so guilty about it. The little bunkin was about to give up when he felt another unmistakable niggle in his tummy. He remembered his old friend, the one who had told him that he was braver than he knew. The one who had believed in him from the very beginning. 'Horatio once told me . . .' he began, feeling a stab of longing in his heart.

At the mention of that name, everyone stared at Shylo. Horatio was Nelson's brother and a veteran Royal Rabbit who had nearly been killed by the corgis, but had miraculously escaped and vanished to the countryside to live in hiding. His bravery commanded respect. When Shylo was living in the Warren with his mother and siblings, he had become friends with Horatio and it was the elderly rabbit who had sent Shylo to find the Royal Rabbits when the Queen had been in danger.

'Horatio once told me—' Shylo repeated.

At that moment, the big doors opened and a gruff voice interrupted. 'Always listen to a niggle,' it said.

The eyes fixed on Shylo switched suddenly to the large buck now hopping stiffly into the room. He was huge, with coarse grey fur and a long scar down one side of his face. His left ear had been almost entirely bitten off and he was missing a hind paw. He leaned heavily on a walking stick. He looked as if he had once been in a terrible fight and had only just survived.

The Hopsters stared at the buck in bewilderment. Where was Frisby, the Major-domo? She always announced visitors with three knocks on the big doors. How had this stranger got past security and into The Grand Burrow? He looked vaguely familiar, but who was he?

However, Nelson knew and so did Shylo.

'Horatio!' cried the little bunny, so excited to see his old friend again that he forgot he was a Royal Rabbit and bounded over and threw his arms round the buck's waist.

'Brother!' murred Nelson in surprise.

Horatio laughed as Shylo's grip tightened round

him. 'Yes, one must always listen to a niggle!' he said, patting the bunkin tenderly.

Laser, Clooney and Zeno looked at one another in amazement. They had heard about the Generalissimo's brother, Horatio, the only rabbit to survive the Kennel, but never imagined he'd come back to The Grand Burrow.

Nelson hopped over to his brother and embraced him. Shylo released Horatio and watched with large, shiny eyes as the two siblings were reunited after many years apart.

'How marvellous to see you, brother! I hoped you'd respond to my letter and come back, but the weeks went by and I heard nothing from you,' gravelled Nelson, patting Horatio's back a little too hard in order to hide his emotion. 'I'm glad you finally decided to return to The Grand Burrow. The Royal Rabbits need you. Times have never been more dangerous.'

The other rabbits queued up to shake his paw, but the gruff Horatio would have none of this.

'Enough. I didn't come back to shake paws. I came back because—' But he was interrupted.

'Forgive my rudeness, but I'm Marshal of the Thumpers,' bellowed Zeno, 'and I'd like to know how you got past security and into The Grand Burrow!'

'I know the old craft of the Secret Service,' replied Horatio in a slow and deliberate voice. 'I'm an ancient rabbit from the Old World. I know tunnels beneath the palace that you youngsters have never heard of. But let's not waste time. I came back because I read about the stolen diamond in the newspapers and thought you might need my help.'

'Go on,' said Nelson as the other rabbits listened attentively.

'Many years ago, when I was working for the SRS - the Secret Rabbit Service - I was assigned a covert mission and travelled to Russia. I spent enough time there to learn their language and their ways. No one knows more about Russia and its people than me. No one knows more about the Minks of the Kremlin than me either. No one has ever got as close. So I decided it was time to come back.'

He settled his wise old eyes on Shylo and smiled affectionately. 'This little bunkin taught me a valuable lesson about bravery. I never thought I'd return to The Grand Burrow. After being caught by the Pack and nearly eaten in the Kennel, I didn't think I'd find the courage.'

He lifted his right paw, which was wrapped in a bandage, and slowly unwound the fabric. The rabbits watched in fascination, wondering what he was going to reveal. At last, the bandage fell away and there, in bright scarlet, was the Badge of the Royal Rabbits of London, which he had concealed during his years in hiding. He was hiding no more.

'Thanks to Shylo,' he said, 'I found my courage. Here I am, at your service.'

'And we're happy to have you,' murred Nelson. 'You have arrived when you are most needed. Perhaps you felt a niggle too?'

'Well, I suppose I had a niggle of sorts. You see, when I learned that the diamond had been stolen, my thoughts immediately turned to the Russians . . .'

'As did ours,' agreed Zeno triumphantly. He always liked to be right.

'My thoughts also turned to the most fearsome mink in the whole of Russia. I believe I am the only Royal Rabbit to have ever met him.'

The Royal Rabbits glanced at each other uneasily.

'Who is he?' Nelson asked.

Horatio looked at them in turn. Then he lifted his chin and said, in a deep, gravelly voice, 'Minsky-the-

Terrible.'

Shylo's fur stood on end. The name sounded . . .
TERRIBLE.

'Now, what time is it?' Horatio asked.

Nelson looked at the clock on the wall. 'Seven thirty
a.m.'

'Perfect. Get me to Kensington Gardens at once!'
said Horatio. 'If I'm right, I know just where to find
those minks.

'And, if Minsky-the-Terrible is with them, I'm the
only one who can identify him!'

CHAPTER FIVE

Not long afterwards, an old lady in a wheelchair was being pushed by her nurses down the Broad Walk of Kensington Gardens. If one looked closely, one might have noticed that, under her hat, the old lady had whiskers and a pink nose (but then old ladies can sometimes have whiskers and a pink nose, can't they?) and that the two nurses pushing the chair were ill-matched: one was enormous with bulging muscles under her nurse's uniform and the other was tiny with a red eyepatch - and both had ears tucked under headscarves. Yes, the trio were of course Horatio in a cunning disguise being cared for by Zeno the Thumper and Shylo the bunkin.

Luckily, because it was so early, there were only a few humans in the park and they were far too busy hurrying through it on their way to work to pay any attention to the strange old lady and her companions.

'Quick! Wheel me towards Kensington Palace,' Horatio demanded. 'Chop-chop.'

Zeno and Shylo pushed him so fast they were soon speeding down the hill, past the golden gates of Kensington Palace. Suddenly, Horatio shouted, 'Slow down! There! Look!'

A short distance away, on the grass, just beside the little gate which led to Millionaires' Row and the Russian Embassy, they saw what looked like a group of children in white judo pyjamas doing t'ai-chi exercises in perfect unison beneath the trees. At first, Shylo

thought they were children, but then, as he narrowed his eyes and focused harder, he realized that they weren't humans at all, but a group of minks.

'I knew it,' muttered Horatio. 'They always used to practise here in the park, beneath the trees. After all these years, their habits haven't changed. Push me along. Slowly. I want to get a little closer.'

'They look like ninnies,' commented Zeno, unimpressed.

'They might look like that to you, but they're extremely dangerous! Each one is a highly trained killer,' Horatio told him sternly.

Shylo couldn't help but agree with Zeno: the minks didn't look as scary as he'd thought they would. They were performing their exercises with the grace of dancers.

'Now, let me see . . .' murmured Horatio.

Slowly, they wheeled the old buck's chair towards

the minks and, as they did so, the Russian animals divided into pairs and started judo fighting, slicing at each other with a chopping action and throwing one another on to the grass.

'Five pairs. One instructor. Yes, one judo master,' Horatio murred, almost to himself, scratching his chin thoughtfully. He concentrated on the black-belted instructor who whispered orders and was instantly obeyed.

Suddenly, the instructor moved so fast that he became a blur of brown and white. He threw every one of the minks on to the grass before Shylo could blink.

'Ah yes. As I thought,' said Horatio. He turned to Shylo and Zeno. 'I've seen all I need to see. Now we must return to The Grand Burrow.'

Zeno let out a big sigh. He wasn't enjoying this mission one bit. He did not like dressing up as a nurse and he did not want to be pushing Horatio in a wheelchair. He sighed again and shoved the chair with a grunt.

But Shylo was curious. 'What did you see back there, Horatio?' he asked.

'It's him,' Horatio replied. 'It's been thirty years since I met him, but I'd know him anywhere. The black moustache is grey now, but *that* was Minsky-the-Terrible. I'd bet my life on it. He's here and that's not good news.'

Shylo glanced back at the group of minks. He felt very frightened. Minsky sounded quite awful. Keen to get away as quickly as possible, Shylo pushed the wheelchair much too fast, almost spilling Horatio on to the Broad Walk as they hurried back to The Grand Burrow.

'Easy, Shylo!' exclaimed Zeno, sensing the bunkin's panic. 'No one's going to hurt you while you're with me.'

As soon as they reported back in the map room, Zeno announced, 'Just say the word, Generalissimo, and I will ready the Thumpers to storm the embassy. If Minsky-the-Terrible is here and he's as fierce as Horatio says he is, then it can mean one thing and one thing only: the Russians have the Siberian Diamond.'

However, Shylo put his paw on his belly, where his niggle still niggled, and thought, *But do they?*

CHAPTER SIX

In a sumptuous mansion in Hampstead (a suburb of North London inhabited by a species that a scientist might call *humanus richus*), Amura, the fat white Siberian tigress, was surfing through fashion websites on her laptop. She was clicking with her mouse, buying more designer dresses, perfumes, shoes and handbags from the most expensive shops. All day and all night, new deliveries arrived at the mansion.

Amura's owner was an eccentric Russian billionairess who loved to collect exotic animals. She kept the tiger in her luxurious London home, but, because the billionairess had houses all over the world, she rarely came to check on her pet tiger and Amura had taken over the mansion, treating it as her own palace, naming it Tiger Towers and spending her owner's money on the internet.

In the grand master bedroom, Amura was surrounded by a trio of she-wolves, called tundra wolves. They had thick white fur, bright sapphire-blue eyes, sharply pointed ears and long noses that sloped up at the end. These wolves looked after Amura's every need. They served her, pampered her and protected her and never complained, even though she was a very demanding tigress!

At this moment, one was painting liquid gold on to the claws of Amura's right hind paw, while another served her favourite delicacy: deliciously light and fluffy powder-pink marshmallows, which she ate sprinkled with black caviar from the Caspian Sea. The third tundra wolf was unpacking the items that Amura had ordered on the internet, holding up new pairs of shoes, dresses and sunglasses for her boss to inspect.

'Keep that! Send that back!' Amura was saying as she viewed her shopping. While this was going on she was covered in thick bleaching foam, because Amura was actually a yellow tiger and had to dye her yellow fur white because she had watched a documentary on television about white tigers and thought they were much rarer and more glamorous than yellow ones. (At one point, she had wanted to be pink to match her marshmallows, but the tundra wolves had managed to talk her out of it.) Her hairdresser, a manicured lilac poodle who was owned by the proprietor of a beauty salon on the high street, was putting the lids on the tubes of dye she had stolen from the salon while she waited for the bleach to work its magic.

Now only Amura's eyes were visible, blinking through two holes in the froth, and she was *very* pleased with her eyes, for they were a rare and beautiful green, the colour of pistachios. She did *not* need to dye them.

A string trio of blind moles had been hired to play disco music on electric bubblegum-pink violins, but Amura shushed them as her attention was drawn to the huge TV screen in the centre of the room. A newsflash was reporting that the famous Siberian Diamond had been stolen from Buckingham Palace. The reporter said that the police suspected that the Russian Secret Service had stolen it on behalf of the Kremlin, for the Russians had been demanding its return for the last one hundred years. But the Russians were denying they had anything to do with the theft and the President himself had sent a message of sympathy to the King and Queen, promising to do all he could to help find it.

However, Amura knew the police were wrong. Oh, how she revelled in their ignorance! She chewed her marshmallow and caviar and smacked her lips.

You see, the Russian Secret Service hadn't stolen the diamond; *she* had. Well, to be more accurate, her three cunning tundra wolves had stolen it for her because Amura was much too lazy to sneak into Buckingham Palace. 'Bring me the Siberian Diamond or I'll eat you!' she had told them.

Why did Amura want the diamond so badly, you may ask. Amura had plenty of jewels for she was rich, *very* rich, on account of having remembered all the numbers of her owner's credit cards (Amura had a very good memory). But the trouble with rich people is that they can never be rich enough. They *always* want just a little bit more. There is *always* someone richer and they *always* want what that someone has,

even if it's the Queen!

In Tiger Towers, everything was white apart from the indoor swimming pool, which was black and decorated with a mosaic of a white tiger on the bottom. Amura filled the house with every kind of luxury. She had all that money could buy, but she had grown bored and dissatisfied, because material things do not bring lasting happiness. One grows tired of them very quickly and starts to feel empty and craving more. But Amura didn't know this, which is why she decided she must have the Siberian Diamond, the most beautiful jewel of all, because it was one thing she couldn't have (and greedy creatures like Amura always want what they can't have). She had seen a photograph of it in a magazine while she was having her fur dyed and decided that, as it came from Siberia like she did, she really ought to own it. Only the Siberian Diamond could make her happy, she believed. But, so far, it had not made her as happy as she'd thought it would. Something was making her discontented, but she couldn't think what it was.

When her nails had dried and her fur was the colour of snow, the hairdresser left and Amura wandered into her dressing room to decide what to wear. She took a long time flicking through the rails of hanging outfits. There were rows and rows of shelves, and cupboards full of clothes and shoes and handbags, and every item showed the label of the shop it had come from. Amura's favourite shop was the ridiculously expensive Jazz Tiger, and most of her clothes displayed the JT logo in big gold letters for everyone to see. Even the towels in her bathrooms had huge JT logos emblazoned on them. Once she'd chosen her outfit, a shimmering metallic evening gown in the brightest silver, she wandered back into her bedroom.

At last, she stood in front of the magnificent Siberian Diamond, displayed in a shiny glass cabinet against the wall near her bed, so that when she woke up in the morning and went to sleep at night it was the first and last thing she saw.

The tigress rubbed her polished paws together and her chubby cheeks creased as she smiled. But her smile wasn't as wide as it should have been. Her three tundra wolves stood beside her in tight black jumpsuits with gold belts around their waists, and gazed at the diamond they had stolen for their mistress.

'It's more beautiful than the moon,' gushed Sapphire.

'More beautiful than the sun,' enthused Lapis.

'More beautiful than the stars,' exclaimed Topaz.

'But less beautiful than *me*!' purred Amura in a little cub voice, and she wasn't joking.

'Of course, Amura. Nothing in the world is more

beautiful than you!' the wolves replied in unison. They knew how to flatter their mistress.

Amura huffed and suddenly looked deeply unhappy. She popped a deliciously light and fluffy powder-pink marshmallow into her mouth. 'I thought stealing the diamond would make me happy. But what good is it if no one knows I have it?' she complained.

'But Amura, if the Russian Secret Service know you have it, they will try to take it from you,' said Sapphire sensibly.

'If the *British* Secret Service know you have it, *they* will try to steal it back as well,' warned Topaz.

'But I want everyone to know how clever I am,' Amura wheedled in a sulky voice.

The wolves glanced at each other nervously.

'And I want everyone to know how *rich* I am. Now that I have the priceless Siberian Diamond, I am richer than everyone else in the whole wide world. But what's the point if I can't show it off?'

At last, she had reached the core of her discontentment. She would only be truly happy if *everyone knew she had the diamond!*

Now the wolves began to look really uneasy. When Amura wanted something, she usually got it. The something that Amura wanted now was not, they knew, a good idea. However, they were not paid to advise but to act upon her every wish, so, if Amura insisted, there would be nothing they could do to dissuade her - after all, they didn't want to be eaten.

'How about we make a deal with the Ratzis?' Amura suggested, tossing another caviar-sprinkled marshmallow into her mouth.

Sapphire's jaw fell open in horror. Lapis gasped and Topaz snarled, baring sharp white teeth. Normally, wolves are not afraid of rats; however, Ratzis, as I'm sure you know, are not ordinary rats: they are giant super-rats who work for the world's biggest internet company run by the mysterious Papa Ratzi. 'The Big Ratzi', as he was also known, would have loved to learn that Amura had stolen the diamond so that he could publish the *real* story in his newspapers and prove everyone else wrong.

Sapphire thought of the greasy, smelly, junk-food-eating Ratzis and turned up her snout. 'You can't trust Ratzis, Amura.'

Amura smiled the sly, greedy smile of a tigress who is never satisfied. 'But if I just let them know that I *might* have the diamond,' she purred.

'I'm not su—' began Lapis.

'WHAT IS THE POINT OF HAVING IT IF NO ONE KNOWS I'VE GOT IT!' roared Amura. The wolves jumped in alarm, for when Amura roared, it was thunderous.

The Siberian tigress chewed another marshmallow

and added, more softly, 'The Russians might have it or I might have it, but no one will know for sure, will they?' She turned to Lapis, her expression deadly serious. 'Let's give them a clue. Set up a meeting with a Ratzi. This is going to be fun!'

A short while later, in a damp alleyway in Central London, a fat, greasy rat with a jutting jaw and a dribbling loose lip (which was the result of a fight she had had with a vicious badger - and won) stood waiting for the mystery animal who had requested a meeting with her, promising a scoop.

Slippery Mavis was awful, even for a Ratzi. Her belly bulged from all the junk food she ate, her bottom let out terrible farts because of the fizzy drinks she drank and her breath was so stinky that flies died in mid-air if they flew within a few metres of her.

But Mavis was ambitious. She wanted Papa Ratzi to be pleased with her, because if he was he might reward her by making her famous. He might even give her her own reality TV show! After all, once, when a rat had pleased Papa Ratzi, he had granted her a wish. (That rat had only requested a holiday in the sewer - Mavis would ask for more, *much* more.) She craved fame more than anything in the world. She wanted to be a celebrity, and she'd do anything to be one.

If this scoop turned out to be a delicious scandal, Papa Ratzi would be *very* pleased with her indeed! So she waited in the rain, smartphone in one hand, tablet in the other, because while she had time to kill she might as well play a few games.

Suddenly, a lithe and agile creature bounded down the alleyway and came to an abrupt stop before her. It was dressed completely in black - black jumpsuit, black boots, black gloves and a black mask - and

Slippery Mavis wasn't even able to tell what sort of animal it was. But she could see that it was very tall and slim and powerful. Mavis did not want to get into a fight with this creature, whatever it was.

'What have you got?' Mavis asked as a drop of drool slipped from her lip and plopped on to the wet cobbles by her hind paws. The creature pulled an envelope out of its breast pocket. 'What's this?' Mavis asked, snatching it out of the gloved paw. But, before Mavis had time to open the envelope and look inside, the mysterious creature had darted away, like a sprite into the darkness.

Slippery Mavis snarled furiously. There was no explanation. Not so much as a 'hello'. Yet she was curious to see what was in the envelope. *Better not look at it in the rain*, she thought. *I'll wait until I get back to Rat Central.* She put it in her rucksack, pulled out a rotten tuna sandwich she'd found in the park that afternoon and took a bite. The tuna was off and the bread was stale, just how she liked them. She licked her chops and made her way back to the Shard.

CHAPTER SEVEN

Ratzi HQ is situated at the top of the Shard, the tallest building in London. The tower rises into the sky like a giant needle, piercing the clouds. And now Mavis was standing on the roof of the lift, waiting for an oblivious human to step inside and press the button so she could make her way to the very top. It wasn't long before a man in a suit with a briefcase strode in and did just that, little knowing that a fat, stinky rat was right above him.

With a *whoosh*, the lift went up, stopping at one or

two floors to let people in and out, until it reached Mavis's destination: the top floor. She hopped on to a ledge and scaled a rope the final few metres to the gleaming offices of Papa Ratzi's London base, which were situated in the very highest point of the building, almost in the clouds. Out of breath and panting, because Ratzis are very unfit (they HATE exercise even more than they hate healthy food), Mavis staggered into the hall.

You may be surprised to learn that, although Ratzis like eating rotten food (the stinkier the better), their offices are not dirty and dingy like the places rats usually inhabit. That is because Ratzis are way more intelligent and far more dangerous than normal rats, so instead of rootling through rubbish and scuttling around underground they make the world an uglier place by spreading lies and hate on the internet. Rat Central is bright and clean with vast, shiny windows that look out over the whole of London. It is full of offices with desks and chairs and the most up-to-date computers, smartphones and laptops. Giant screens broadcast news from a thousand channels and internetworks run by Papa Ratzi.

Papa Ratzi himself has never visited the Shard. He communicates with his Ratzis by email and text. There is much debate among the Ratzis as to what Papa Ratzi looks like. They imagine him to be monstrously big and terrifyingly strong. If only they knew the truth as we do. That he is a small, pink, ex-laboratory rat, with no fur and big, bulging, cloudy purple eyes, who lives in a cage in a family home in California.

Mavis was keen to keep the envelope she had been given in the alley to herself. She ignored the other Ratzis who tried to talk to her and scuttled furtively to her desk, which was right beside Flintskin's. Flintskin and Mavis sometimes worked together on assignments from Papa Ratzi, but Mavis disliked Flintskin because he always had one eye on her (like an annoying classmate who tries to copy his neighbour in exams). He was just as mean and sneaky as Mavis and had two enormous front teeth that stuck out like a pair of tusks.

Mavis plonked her big, flabby bottom on her chair and pulled out the envelope.

'What's that?' asked Flintskin, peering over her shoulder.

Mavis grimaced. 'Never you mind!'

'Who gave it to you?'

'If you don't mind your own business, I'll thump you!' she snapped.

Flintskin huffed crossly and turned his attention back to his laptop.

'Here, have the rest of this,' said Mavis, handing him the toughest, smelliest and mouldiest piece of

tuna sandwich she had been saving for later.

It was a small sacrifice to distract Flintskin and it worked. He immediately forgot about the mysterious envelope and grabbed the sandwich, stuffing it into his mouth with relish, and chewing greedily. He sighed and he moaned; he gasped and he groaned. It was delicious!

Mavis tore open the envelope and pulled out a photograph. It was a picture of an enormous diamond in a glass cabinet. She instantly recognized it as the stolen Siberian Diamond. But *everyone* knew about that. It had been all over the news!

She clicked her tongue and glared at it crossly. What was so interesting about a photograph of the diamond? There were literally *hundreds* of them on the internet already. Mavis was so furious her time had been wasted that she didn't take the trouble to look at it more closely. Instead, she scowled. What was that creature thinking, giving her a silly old photograph that was no use at all? It didn't tell her who had the diamond or why they had stolen it. It told her nothing at all. Angrily, she tossed the photo into the bin and went  to help herself to a fizzy drink out of the office Grub Cupboard.

As she walked off, Flintskin stopped chewing and looked into the bin. Glancing quickly in the direction of the Grub Cupboard to see if Mavis was coming back, and seeing that she was busily guzzling her fizzy drink and paying no attention to him at all, he cautiously put his sticky paw into the bin and pulled out the photograph. He placed it on his desk and looked at it closely. He saw the diamond and the glass cabinet like Mavis had, but then Flintskin noticed something else: the faint but unmistakable reflection of a white tiger in the glass.

Flintskin's black heart gave a leap. It leaped so hard it thumped against his ribcage like a piece of coal. This photograph was obviously important. He didn't know who the tiger was, but he was certain that Papa Ratzi would. This was his chance to get one up on Mavis and make the Big Ratzi proud! His paws were shaking so much with excitement that he was barely able to type an email to Papa Ratzi. Hastily, he took a photo of the image and attached it to his email before pressing SEND.

It didn't take long for a reply to come.

HA HA HA HA HA! WELL DONE, FLINTSKIN. THIS IS
A REAL SCOOP! SO AMURA, THE WHITE SIBERIAN
TIGER, HAS STOLEN THE DIAMOND, THE FAT CAT!
THIS PROVES THAT THE RUSSIANS WEREN'T
BEHIND THE THEFT AFTER ALL! BUT LET'S
CREATE SOME MAYHEM! SEND THAT PHOTOGRAPH TO
MINSKY-THE-TERRIBLE AT ONCE. MY INTELLIGENCE
HAS INFORMED ME THAT HE IS AT THE RUSSIAN
EMBASSY IN KENSINGTON. LET'S SEE IF HE IS AS
CLEVER AS YOU ARE. IF HE IS, HIS MINKS MIGHT
TAKE THE OPPORTUNITY TO STEAL INTO TIGER
TOWERS AND GET THE DIAMOND FOR THE PRESIDENT
OF RUSSIA. ONCE IT IS BACK IN MOSCOW, WE WILL
PUBLISH THE NEWS ALL OVER THE INTERNET. THE
PRIME MINISTER WILL BE FURIOUS. THE KING
AND QUEEN WILL BE FURIOUS TOO. THIS MIGHT
EVEN LEAD TO WAR BETWEEN RUSSIA AND BRITAIN.
WOULDN'T THAT BE AWESOME!

You can see how diabolically the mind of Papa Ratzi worked.

Flintskin wasted no time in emailing the photograph to the minks at the Russian Embassy. Once he had done it, he was very pleased with himself, and, imagining the reward Papa Ratzi was going to give him, he stood on his chair and did the war dance of the Ratzis, known as a Driggle. He wiggled his wrinkly bottom and waved his long, greasy tail in the air like a lasso. The other Ratzis stopped what they were doing and stared at him suspiciously. What was he so pleased about?

Mavis was drawn away from the Grub Cupboard by the sound of Flintskin singing as he driggled. She made her way slowly to her desk. Flintskin was grinning at her, a grin so wide and happy that it put fear into her heart. She dropped her gaze to the bin. The *empty bin*. Where was the photograph?

Then she saw it on Flintskin's desk.

She stared at Flintskin in alarm. What had she missed? She hadn't seen anything of interest in the photograph at all! But, just as she was about to bash him with her claw, there came the soft lullaby music 'Rock-a-bye Baby' which was the sound of Papa Ratzi's incoming texts.

The Ratzis turned their attention to the rolling hologram of words that now appeared in the air, as if by magic.

FLINTSKIN HAS DISCOVERED WHO HAS THE
DIAMOND. WELL DONE, FLINTSKIN. YOU WILL
RECEIVE A BIG REWARD...

Mavis lunged at Flintskin, claws raised, teeth bared,
but Flintskin was too quick for her. He leaped from
desk to desk so that Mavis had to chase him around
the office. What made her crosser than anything was
the way he paused every now and then to driggle, just
for her.

Deep beneath the Russian Embassy in Kensington,
Minsky-the-Terrible was in the *banya* (which is what
the Russians call a bath house), sitting in a cloud of
steam, when he heard a ping on his smartphone.

Normally, he would not have looked at his phone
while in the *banya* - the *banya* is a place of relaxation

- but, since the Siberian Diamond had been stolen, the Russian President had started fretting: what if the diamond was to fall into the wrong hands? This was Russia's chance to get it back. Minsky sensed the text might be important and thought he'd better take a look.

Due to the warm steam Minsky had felt very relaxed, but now he was agitated. He feared that he would be called into action, because in his day there had been no mink more terrible than him. But he was old now and his terrible days were over. However, in spite of that, he was, undeniably, a little tempted to get involved (he liked the idea of the glory of bringing the diamond home to Russia), but the truth was he was *not* in London for the diamond. He had long retired from working for the Kremlin and was in fact here for a prestigious judo competition. Being a competitive mink, he was determined his team should win. He was not at all happy that the diamond had been stolen at the very same moment that he and his team had come over to London to compete. It wasn't good for their concentration to be distracted by such a drama.

Reluctantly, he delved into the pocket of his dressing gown that hung on a hook on the wall and pulled out his phone.

When he saw that there was an email from Rat Central, he opened it with interest.

He looked at the photograph of the diamond attached to the email and immediately saw a grinning white tiger's face in the reflection of the glass cabinet (minks have little eyes as sharp as needles, like their teeth). 'Well, well, well,' he mumbled in surprise. 'If it isn't our old friend Amura. Who'd have thought it?' He clicked his paws and the other minks who were wallowing in the baths and sweating in the steam rooms stopped what they were doing and hastily gathered round. 'Get dressed,' he ordered. 'We're not practising judo this evening. We're going to Hampstead!'

Judo can wait, he thought with mounting excitement. *This is just too tempting to resist.*

Flintskin's driggling was very annoying, but Slippery Mavis was not called Slippery Mavis for nothing. She was cunning and clever and, as soon as she found out that Papa Ratzi had ordered Flintskin to email the photograph to Minsky-the-Terrible, she decided to ruin their plan. While Flintskin was distracted, doing the Ratzi war dance on the desk while the rest of the Ratzis danced with him, she slipped on to his chair and put her sticky claws on his keyboard. Licking her chops with glee, she sent a copy of the photograph to The Grand Burrow – on Flintskin's computer.

If those Royal Rabbits get their hands on the diamond, they'll give it back to the Queen and that will make Papa Ratzi very cross, she thought to herself cheerfully. *So cross that he won't reward Flintskin after all. In fact, when he finds out that the email was sent to The Grand Burrow on Flintskin's computer, he might lop off his ear instead.* She began to laugh. She laughed so loudly that her flabby belly wobbled like a jelly.

Flintskin glanced back at her and his face darkened with concern.

But it was too late.

Mavis had already pressed SEND.

CHAPTER EIGHT

Deep beneath The Grand Burrow, Rappaport, the bald-headed, blotchy computer expert rabbit, dressed in a three-piece pinstriped suit and a grubby shirt, which had once been white, was on duty in the lair. He was watching his screens in the security room, rubbing the scurf off his flaky pink head and picking his nose, when he suddenly saw the email from Rat Central. Breathing heavily, he hurried up the tunnels to the great hall, then on up the winding staircase towards Nelson's war room.

Frisby, the Major-domo, red-faced and pompous, stopped him with her big staff. 'The Generalissimo is in a meeting with the Hopsters, Rappaport. Come back later,' she said.

'Announce me at once,' Rappaport demanded, wiping his sweaty brow with a grubby handkerchief. 'This is an emergency.'

Frisby huffed crossly, but she banged her staff three times against the double doors, opened them and announced in a high, operatic voice, 'Rappaport, Generalissimo. Apparently, it's an "emergency".'

The scruffy, paunchy rabbit hopped into the room in a state of high excitement. His glasses had misted up, he had an orange stain on his tie and he was twitching more than usual.

'What have you got for me?' Nelson asked.

'Generalissimo, I have just received an email from Rat Central,' he said.

Nelson raised his eyebrows. 'Rat Central?' he repeated in surprise.

'It's a photograph of the diamond. Here, I've printed it out for you.'

He placed it on Nelson's desk. The old buck looked at it and then he laughed. A deep belly laugh that roused the other rabbits' curiosity and sent them hopping over to his desk to see what was so amusing. Laser and Clooney could see it easily, but little Shylo was straining until Zeno lifted him off the ground so that his hind paws dangled in the air. Even Horatio pushed himself up from his comfortable armchair and limped across the floor to join them.

When Shylo saw the photograph, he immediately spotted the tiger's face in the glass. He might have been a weak and feeble bunkin, but he was very clever and quick-witted.

'Mystery solved!' said Clooney with a laugh. 'Looks

like it wasn't the minks behind the theft after all but a tiger!'

Shylo's ears stood up straight. His niggle had been right. It wasn't the Russians! 'Who is this tiger?' he asked as Zeno put him down.

'Rappaport?' said Nelson.

The mangy buck shrugged apologetically. 'I've run a facial recognition program, but have come up with nothing,' he replied.

Belle de Paw studied the photograph carefully. 'I bet she's not a white tiger at all but a yellow one,' she trilled. 'No tiger is *that* white!'

Horatio stepped forward and tapped his walking stick a couple of times on the floor. 'That, my friends, is Amura. I'd recognize her face anywhere.' The Royal Rabbits stared at him in surprise.

'Are you telling me that you know this tiger?' demanded Zeno.

'If I had had the misfortune of knowing her, I would not be standing here now. Tigers like to eat rabbits,' Horatio replied.

'Who is she?' Nelson asked.

'She's a white Siberian tigress and belongs to a very wealthy Russian woman who likes to collect exotic animals. She lives in a very big house in Hampstead called Tiger Towers. It won't be difficult to find. She has Siberian wolves as well, which are very fierce. I would not like to meet them on a dark night.'

'How do you know about this tiger?' Laser asked curiously - after all, it had been many years since Horatio had been in Moscow.

Horatio chuckled and he looked down at Shylo and winked. 'I know because I have had endless hours in the countryside to read. You see, one learns a great deal from reading, as Shylo will tell you.' The little rabbit felt his chest expand with pride.

'You read about Amura in a book?' said Zeno, crinkling his nose because Zeno rarely read anything.

'I read about Amura in a newspaper,' Horatio corrected him. 'There was once a big article about her owner, the Russian billionairess, in *The Times*. I was intrigued.'

'Very well,' said Nelson. 'If she does indeed have the diamond, I suppose it's in Hampstead. But why would the Ratzis want to help us?'

'They don't,' said Clooney. 'Ratzis want to create havoc.'

'It doesn't make sense,' Zeno boomed.

'It sure doesn't!' agreed Laser.

'It's a trap,' said Belle de Paw.

Nelson rubbed his chin thoughtfully. 'If the Ratzis want to create havoc, why not simply inform Minsky-the-Terrible that Amura has the diamond?' he wondered aloud. 'The minks steal it back, the diamond goes to Moscow and the good relationship between Britain and Russia is put in peril. Papa Ratzi would love Britain to be furious with Russia. Peace is what he hates the most.'

'There is only one thing to do,' Belle de Paw suggested with growing excitement. 'We go to Amura's house and find out.'

'Yes!' enthused Zeno, who loved action more than anything. 'Just say the word, Generalissimo, and I'll send my Thumpers into battle.'

Shylo glanced at Horatio who was deep in thought. His face was serious and worried. The little bunny felt anxiety build in his belly.

Nelson nodded. 'You're right, Zeno. Even though we don't know the Ratzis' plans, we need to get the diamond back as soon as possible. I want all my Thumpers to go to Hampstead at once . . .'

Horatio put up a paw, which silenced the room. 'I

would advise caution, Nelson,' he warned. 'The Ratzis' plot is sure to be diabolical. We mustn't fall into a trap.'

'Leave the strategy to me, brother,' said Nelson. 'It's been years since you were in The Grand Burrow and in much of that time I have stood behind this desk and given the orders.'

Horatio shook his head. He looked down at Shylo, who gazed up at him with wide, fearful eyes. Shylo agreed with his old friend: something wasn't right at all. Surely the Ratzis would rather the diamond went to the minks than the rabbits?

Nelson turned to his Hopster rabbits. 'Zeno, I need you to surround the property. Clooney, Shylo and Laser, I want you to find a way into Amura's mansion and bring back the diamond.'

'And me?' asked Belle de Paw. 'I should go too. No one knows more about diamonds than me!'

'I want you at the periscopes, Belle de Paw. I need to know everyone who comes and goes from the palace.'

'But–'

'No discussion, Belle. You are assigned the job you do best, here in The Grand Burrow. I cannot have everyone out in the field.'

Belle de Paw pursed her lips and scowled.

Just then, Shylo's stomach made a loud moaning noise.

'Is that a niggle or a rumble?' Nelson asked.

'A rumble,' Shylo replied, not entirely sure (as I told you, it's difficult to tell).

'Then first you must eat,' said Nelson, glancing at the bunkin who was peeping over the side of the desk with large, hungry eyes. 'There's no point going into battle on an empty stomach!'

While they dined on celery soup, parsnip pie and carrot crumble, Horatio whispered into Shylo's ear: 'I sense there's more to this than anyone has imagined.'

'Is it sure to be a trap?' Shylo asked, feeling a lot better now that his belly was full.

'Most likely,' the old buck replied. 'If the Ratzis have sent that photograph to us, they will most certainly have sent it to Minsky-the-Terrible as well. Go with your eyes open, Shylo. If you expect a trap, you can avoid it. You must use what you think are your disadvantages to your advantage.'

Shylo frowned.

'You are small; the Hopsters are big and tall. They don't have noses as sensitive as yours and you are curious and keen to learn while the Hopsters think they know everything. And remember the most important thing of all I taught you.'

'What's that?' Shylo's ears stood to attention.

'Life is an adventure. Anything in the world is possible - by will and by luck, with a moist carrot, a wet nose and a slice of mad courage! You are braver than you know.'

It was late afternoon when Clooney, Laser, Shylo, Zeno and his Thumpers took the underground cart to Hampstead Heath, emerging near the Ladies' Pond. As they set off, Shylo caught a brief whiff of Belle de Paw's exotic perfume and he hoped she wasn't cross that Nelson had not allowed her to come with them.

The wind ruffled Shylo's fur as the cart rattled swiftly along the railway tracks. As they sped in a northerly direction, his legs began to feel weak and his ears went droopy, flying out behind him. He didn't want to look scared, but, as much as he tried, he could not get his ears to stand up straight. However, he had no desire to stay in The Grand Burrow. He wanted to get the diamond back, because it had been his fault that it was stolen in the first place and he still felt sick every time he thought of it. Yet he was terrified. He just hoped that, when the moment came, Horatio was right and that, somehow, he'd be braver than he knew.

CHAPTER NINE

Minsky-the-Terrible and his special commando unit of minks, all sleek brown fur and white judo pyjamas, climbed out of their black van and approached the grand white Tiger Towers mansion. Silky, serpentine and lithe, they crept along in the shadows, bellies low to the ground, paws padding silently over the pavement, alert to every sound and smell, ready to pounce at any moment.

Minsky was at the front. He was bigger and more muscular than the other minks, and keen to lead the way to find the diamond. He was the strongest mink in the whole of Russia - probably in the whole world. Amura's wolves would surely be no match for him!

The company of minks slid through the black railings that surrounded the property and made their way to the garden at the back of the mansion. Minsky had been there before, by invitation, when Amura had just arrived in London ten years before. She had wanted to maintain a good relationship with Russia in those days and had fed him the most scrumptious feast he had ever had. Who'd have thought a mink would like fluffy powder-pink marshmallows with a sprinkling of caviar?

Hiding in the bushes, he took a silver flask of *kompot* out of the pocket of his judo jacket and had a swig. The sweet Russian drink made of cooked apricots and sour cherries made him feel even stronger. He passed it to the other minks and swept his eyes over the garden, which extended out on to Hampstead Heath.

Just then, Minsky noticed a movement on the heath. He pricked his ears and sniffed the air with his snub nose.

'Royal Rabbits!' he said, picking up their scent. Hastily, he put the flask back in his pocket. 'What are *they* doing here?' he asked. Then he saw, through the darkness, a large number of giant rabbits leaping stealthily over the railings (and one very small one squeezing through). They had reached the mansion not the way Minsky and his company had come, from the front, but from the heath here at the back.

He snarled and said something very rude in Russian, which will not be printed here. 'Have those Ratzis double-crossed me and sent the photo to the pesky Royal Rabbits too?' he smouldered. 'Well, my fellow minks, it seems we may have a fight on our hands.'

Zeno assembled his Thumpers in the bushes at the edge of the garden, facing the mansion. Clooney and Laser checked out the lawn and surrounding shrubbery.

Shylo picked up a strange scent on the wind. It wasn't fox or rabbit but something else entirely. Something he had never smelled before. It had to be the minks. 'We have company,' he said, gingerly poking his nose out of the bush to take a look. 'Minks, I think.'

'Are you sure you're not smelling fox?' Clooney asked him.

'No, this is different,' murred Shylo. The smell seemed to come from the shrubbery to their left. Then he saw them. Shylo shot back into the bush as if something had stung his nose. 'Over th . . . th . . . there!' he stammered in terror.

Zeno leaped out of the bush, followed by Clooney and Laser. Shylo hung back, too afraid to move.

The Hopsters looked at the minks. They didn't look like much, but they knew from Horatio how ferocious they were. It didn't take them long to spot Minsky-the-Terrible. *He* was the biggest and most muscular of them all!

Quickly, Zeno summoned his Thumpers with a flick of his claws. They hopped out of the bushes on to the lawn behind *their* commander.

Minsky in return summoned the minks with a whistle. They took up their judo positions behind their commander.

'Horatio was right - this is a trap!' Laser snapped crossly. 'And we've fallen right into it!'

From the other side of the garden, Minsky scowled. 'This *is* a trap!' he sneered furiously. 'Why did I ever trust a Ratzi?'

Laser nudged Clooney. 'While Zeno keeps the minks busy, let's see if we can find a way into this place.'

'Good idea,' Clooney replied. 'Come on, Shylo, we might find an open window small enough to push you through!'

Shylo's heart began to beat wildly. He didn't think he'd be brave enough to enter that mansion on his own.

'Ears up, Shylo!' Laser exclaimed. 'We have a job to do.' The three of them set off while Zeno stared at Minsky and Minsky stared at Zeno and neither of them moved.

Then suddenly the back door of the fortified mansion opened. Zeno and Minsky turned and watched as two fearsome white wolves in black jumpsuits and gold belts stepped out.

CHAPTER TEN

Shylo, Laser and Clooney snuck round the mansion, trying all the windows, but to no avail. They were all firmly shut. 'There's no way into this place,' complained Clooney. 'It's like a fortress!'

'How about we come down the chimney?' Laser suggested.

'Do I look like Santa Claus?' retorted Clooney crossly. The big buck dropped his gaze on to Shylo. He rubbed his chin. 'Well, you're small enough . . .'

Shylo was not going to go down any chimney, of

that he was certain. He glanced around and spotted a black van parked in the road a short distance from the mansion. On the side of it was a picture of a mink in judo pyjamas and the words: *Minsky's Martial Arts Club.* His ears stiffened with excitement. 'I think I have an idea,' he exclaimed. 'Follow me.'

Clooney looked at Laser and shrugged, but they both knew from experience that Shylo's ideas were rather good. After all, he hadn't been invited to join the Royal Rabbits for nothing. The three rabbits hopped through the black railings surrounding the property and approached the van.

'What is this?' said Clooney, taking in the picture. 'Minsky's Martial Arts Club?'

'Help me open the back?' said Shylo. Clooney, being so much bigger and stronger, pulled the handle and the boot door lifted easily. Inside were piles of white judo pyjamas, all clean and neatly pressed.

Shylo turned to the two Hopsters and grinned. 'I have a plan . . .'

A moment later, Shylo was standing beside Laser and Clooney at the front gates of Amura's mansion. He wanted to at least look brave on the outside, even though he didn't *feel* brave on the inside.

Clooney peered at the guardhouse. It had CCTV cameras outside and special fortified doors. Inside, a huge white wolf was watching a line of TV screens.

Shylo's sensitive nose picked up another unfamiliar smell. It wasn't fox, or rabbit, or even mink. Indeed, it smelled unlike any animal he had ever come across before. It was sweet, like perfume, but not pleasant like Belle de Paw's perfume, and it was filling the air around him.

Suddenly, the door of the guardhouse opened. The wolf gazed at the three rabbits, paws on hips, blue eyes narrowed, pointy ears pricked. 'What have we here?' she growled.

'We're couriers,' said Shylo, lifting his chin and trying to look unafraid. 'We have a package for . . .' He pulled a piece of notepaper from his pocket and pretended to consult it. 'Mrs Amurpha of Tiglet Town - is that your address?'

The wolf glanced at him warily. 'You mean Miss Amura of Tiger Towers! Get the address right, you idiot! Is that your van?' Sapphire pointed at the minks' black vehicle. 'Unload it now!'

Just then, there came a roar from the walkie-talkie at her hip. It was so loud and thunderous that it shook the earth they were standing on. Shylo glanced at Laser; Laser glanced at Clooney; Clooney shrugged.

'SAPPHIRE! THE HAIRDRESSER HAS JUST ARRIVED AT THE STAFF ENTRANCE TO DYE MY TAIL. LET HER IN AT ONCE!' the voice bellowed.

Sapphire was surprised. The hairdresser didn't usually come at this hour. However, she unhooked her walkie-talkie from her gold belt and spoke into it. 'I'll let her in right away, Amura! No problem.' She gave a heavy sigh. She didn't have time to go round to the staff entrance at the side of the mansion and deal with these three rabbits at the same time. What should she do? She couldn't risk Amura getting angry if she was kept waiting . . . So, deciding that the hairdresser visited Tiger Towers often enough to be able to find her way to Amura's bedroom by herself, Sapphire went into the guardhouse and pressed the button to open the staff entrance door remotely.

Goodness, Amura is very tiring to work for, she thought, a little resentfully. *What a demanding diva!*

(Usually, divas scream and shout when they don't get what they want, but this one just threatened to eat you.)

Sapphire turned back to the rabbits. 'You three! Hurry up and get your packages out of the van!'

The three rabbits hopped to the van. They lifted a pile of judo pyjamas out and carried them back to the guardhouse.

'What are they?' Sapphire asked, inspecting them suspiciously. They didn't seem like the usual items Amura ordered online.

'Very chic pyjamas,' said Clooney who looked just the part of a fashion guru in his dinner jacket, red cummerbund and bow tie. 'Very hot right now after the Paris shows!' he added with a grin.

Sapphire huffed impatiently. 'Fine, but we don't need three of you to carry them inside. The pipsqueak can take them in while you other two wait in the van,' she ordered.

Shylo gulped.

'Hurry up, little rabbit!' snapped the wolf. 'I haven't got all day!'

Shylo hopped through the now open gates and paused before the bulletproof doors of Tiger Towers, which looked like a great mouth ready to swallow him whole.

He glanced back at Laser and Clooney one last time. He had no choice now but to be brave. Laser frowned at him anxiously. Clooney gave him a nod of encouragement. Then in he went.

'Will we ever see him again?' Laser wondered fearfully as Shylo disappeared inside.

'If we don't, it's all for King and Queen,' said Clooney, bowing his ears. 'But let's hope he finds the diamond before the Russians do.'

'Right now, I'm not concerned about the diamond,'

said Laser with a sigh. 'I gotta tell you, I'm mighty fond of that bunkin. I sure hope he makes it out in one piece. With or without the jewel.'

Hastily, the two Hopsters hurried back to the garden to see if they could help Zeno and the Thumpers. They expected to come upon a ferocious fight, but to their astonishment Zeno was not in a battle with Minsky-the-Terrible, but being taught judo!

Clooney and Laser stared in amazement. Minsky and Zeno roared with laughter as the little mink threw the huge buck on to the grass as if he weighed no more than a mouse. The Thumpers were looking a little apprehensive as the other minks gave them their own lessons.

'What's going on?' Laser demanded, hopping over to Zeno, who was still lying on his back.

'Well, once we all realized that this was a sneaky Ratzi trap, Minsky and I decided not to give them the

fight they were hoping for,' said Zeno, putting his paw on his stomach and letting out a great belly laugh. 'Instead, Minsky offered to teach me some moves. He's a MONSTER!'

'You have potential, but a lot to learn, big buck!' said Minsky, striking a judo pose.

'This is no time for fooling around, Zeno. Shylo's inside and in great danger,' Clooney interrupted gravely.

'We are not "fooling around",' said Minsky, narrowing his sharp eyes.

'No,' agreed Zeno.

'We're creating a distraction,' Minsky continued.

'What for?' asked Laser, confused. Why would Minsky want to help them?

Minsky shrugged and lowered his voice. 'I'm retired now, my friends. I'm not the spy I once was. I thought I'd come and take a look out of curiosity, but, to be honest with you, I'm not really very interested in stealing the diamond back for Russia. I'd rather do judo and win a gold medal for the motherland!' He glanced at the mansion. 'While your comrade is inside, we might as well keep those two pairs of eyes on *us*, don't you think?'

Laser and Clooney turned to look at the mansion. There, standing in the doorway, were two tundra wolves, looking baffled.

'In that case,' said Laser, thinking of the little bunkin in the mansion and praying that he was all right, 'let's keep them distracted! You might as well teach me too. I've always wanted to know how you guys do that.'

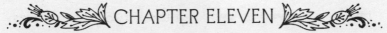 CHAPTER ELEVEN

Meanwhile, inside Tiger Towers, Shylo followed Sapphire across the white marble floor of the hallway.

The doors slowly shut behind him with an ominous click.

Now all he had to do was find the diamond. But how was he going to do that with an enormous tundra wolf by his side?

Amura's mansion was very impressive to a small bunkin like Shylo. It had a spacious hall, gleaming pillars holding up a vaulted ceiling, which was painted to look like a blue sky with white clouds, and big, twinkling chandeliers. Every wall had gold-framed paintings of a smirking white Siberian tiger whom Shylo recognized as Amura from the photo he'd seen. The place seemed empty. It was very quiet.

Suddenly, the sickly-sweet scent he'd smelled outside the mansion filled his nostrils. He spun round.

There, standing in the doorway of one of her magnificent rooms, was Amura herself, dressed in a frilly pink dressing gown and furry pink slippers.

Shylo caught his breath.

He gulped.

He backed away.

But there was nowhere to run. The tundra wolf was behind him and the tiger was blocking his exit with her enormous, fluffy, white-and-black-striped body. Her paws were twice the size of Shylo's entire body.

'Well, well, well,' Amura purred, grinning happily. 'What have we here, Sapphire? A little rabbit?' She stepped closer.

'A courier,' said Sapphire.

'You have a lovely home,' Shylo murred, trying not to look as frightened as he felt.

Amura was pleased. 'You think so?' she purred.

'Oh yes. It's a palace fit for a queen!' he exclaimed, trying to stop his teeth chattering. He didn't want her to realize how terrified he was.

She clapped her paws, drawing Shylo's attention to her painted gold claws. 'I am not a queen, but I do live like one.'

Sensing her vanity, Shylo decided to try to win her over with flattery. 'But you are more *beautiful* than any queen.'

'Amura . . .' Sapphire began, wanting the courier rabbit to hand over his package and leave as quickly

as possible so she could go back and guard the gates.

'Shut up!' growled Amura crossly. Then she smiled at the rabbit. 'You were saying?'

'That you are more beautiful than any queen,' Shylo repeated.

This delighted her. Her pistachio-green eyes gleamed. 'Do you think so?'

'I do. I've never seen a white tiger before.' Well, he hadn't seen any tiger before, so that was true.

Amura shivered with pleasure. 'We are very rare,' she told him. 'There are so few of us around. In fact, there's only one in the entire country, and I am it.'

Just as Shylo was beginning to believe he knew how to handle her, Amura narrowed her eyes and changed from a purring cat to a fearsome tiger. 'Enough about me. Where's my usual courier?' she growled suddenly.

Shylo jumped. His fur stood on end; his knees nearly gave way. But somehow he remained standing.

He took a deep breath and tried to ignore his heart that hammered against his bones.

'I . . . I'm just delivering the pyjamas that you ordered online,' he replied quickly.

'Did I?' she asked, crinkling her nose at the sight of them. 'But they look hideous! And small! They're made for mice not tigers! I'll have to send them back.' She sighed and ran her eyes up and down Shylo, her voice all soft and sweet and purring again. 'It's surprisingly nice to chat to you, little rabbit. A gallant animal who knows how to talk to a lady.'

'A queen,' Shylo corrected, bowing.

'Amura,' said Sapphire, more insistent this time.

Amura glared at her and stamped her hind paw irritably. 'GO BACK OUTSIDE AND DO YOUR JOB, SAPPHIRE!' she roared. She lowered her voice. 'This little rabbit is not going to do any harm, are you, bunnykins?'

The tundra wolf rolled her eyes and left with a huff.

Shylo tried to stop shaking. Amura was the most terrifying creature he had ever encountered. How he wished Clooney and Laser were with him!

Amura laughed, although to Shylo it sounded a lot like a growl. And, as she opened her mouth, he saw her gleaming white and scarily sharp teeth.

'As you're such a gentleman, I'll let you in on a very special secret. I have something that no one else in the world has.'

Shylo tried to hide his surprise. Was Amura going to show him the Siberian Diamond? Surely it couldn't be this easy . . .

Amura motioned with her paw for Shylo to follow her and walked out of the room, her black-and-white tail swaying behind her as she ascended the marble stairs.

'I have the very diamond that once belonged to

Catherine the Great of Russia and the Queen of England,' she boasted as he scampered after her. 'Now it belongs to me.'

'How did you get such a diamond?' Shylo asked.

'Why do you ask?' She glanced at him and Shylo saw the softness in her features very quickly harden again.

'B . . . because I imagine a king must have given it to you. If I were a king, I would give you a diamond as well.'

Her features softened again. 'How sweet you are,' she purred, tracing a gold claw down his cheek.

Shylo held his breath as it went through his fur and grazed his skin. One false move and that claw could do a lot of damage.

'Of course, you're right,' she continued, removing the claw. 'The King of England gave it to me.'

Shylo would normally have bowed his ears at the

mention of the King, but he knew he had to be careful. 'How generous of him,' he said instead.

'I've been keeping it hidden. But, as you're such a lovely bunny, I'll show it to you so that you can admire it.'

Shylo couldn't believe it. Was he really going to be shown the diamond? 'I can't imagine it's more beautiful than you,' he murred, hoping she wouldn't turn nasty again.

She laughed. 'You are so right, my little friend.' She put her paw into her dressing-gown pocket and pulled out a marshmallow. 'These are my favourite things,' she exclaimed, popping the sweet into her mouth and closing her eyes to savour the taste. 'And this is the secret ingredient.' She pulled a tin of caviar out of her other pocket, flicked it open with her claw and dipped another marshmallow into the gleaming black sturgeon eggs. 'Try this!'

Shylo thought it looked revolting, but he knew he couldn't refuse. He took a small bite. The salty-sugary taste spread over his tongue. It was disgusting. The caviar was clammy and cold, the marshmallow sweet and soggy. *Yuck!*

'Hmmmm! Delicious!' he gushed, trying not to gag.

They stood before a big set of double doors with gold knobs. Amura pushed them open to reveal a very fluffy and extremely pink bedroom with a ceiling of disco lights. Shylo spotted a glass cabinet standing against the opposite wall, the same glass cabinet that was in the photograph he had seen in Nelson's war room.

It was EMPTY!

Amura stared at the cabinet in horror.

'WHERE IS MY DIAMOND?' She roared so loudly that the glass in the windows shook. 'MY PRECIOUS DIAMOND!' she ROARED again.

Once more, Shylo could see the sharp teeth in her wide-open mouth. He was so terrified that he couldn't move. He was paralysed, frozen on the spot, as if her roar had turned him to ice. And, before he could work out what was happening, Amura grabbed him with her colossal paw and swung him into the air. His stomach turned as he flew high and then turned again as he landed with a slurp, right in Amura's mouth. Her big white teeth closed behind him and he was faced with the terrifying sight of her pink throat.

This is it, he thought in panic. *This is where it all ends.*

His whole life now passed before his eyes. The Warren where he had grown up. His mother's kisses. Horatio's burrow where the old buck had read him stories of rabbit history. The Weeping Willow. The Grand Burrow. His short time as a Royal Rabbit. His heart filled with a dreadful sorrow.

Not only was Shylo petrified but he felt sick as well. Sick in his stomach because of the marshmallow and caviar. Sick in his heart because he had failed the Royal Rabbits and the King and Queen. And just sick because one never feels very well when one is about to be eaten by a Siberian tiger. Or any tiger, I should imagine.

Just as he was sure he was about to be swallowed, there came another sound. Not a roar or a growl but a deep whimper. Shylo realized, to his amazement, that Amura was sobbing. And one big sob later he felt himself being expelled. He landed on the pink bed with a bounce.

Amura ignored him. Frantically, she began to search her bedroom, lifting everything into the air and throwing it on to the carpet in a rage. She pulled the sheets off the bed and tore open the pillows so that feathers fell all around them like snow. 'WHO HAS

TAKEN MY DIAMOND?' she roared, then sobbed helplessly.

Shylo sat up. His fur was soaking wet from Amura's slobber and he was covered in pillow feathers. He tried to shake them off, but the slobber was acting like glue, and the feathers remained firmly stuck.

Then he got the feeling they were not alone. He lifted his eyes and saw that the bedroom was unexpectedly crowded with creatures:

The tundra wolves were looking at the empty cabinet in horror (and Sapphire was worrying about the hairdresser she had buzzed into the mansion without checking she really was a hairdresser).

Minsky-the-Terrible's mouth had fallen open.

Zeno, Laser and Clooney seemed very relieved to see that Shylo was alive (even though he did look a sorry sight all covered in feathers).

They were all asking themselves the same questions:

where had the diamond gone? Who had snuck in there before them?

Minsky scratched his head. If the rabbits didn't have it, and the minks didn't have it, and Amura didn't have it, then who did?

Shylo's ears flopped over his forehead and he felt a terrible sinking feeling in his stomach where only moments before he had felt sick.

Amura stopped searching the room and turned round to face them.

'Let's get out of here!' cried Minsky. 'Before we're served up as dinner!'

'Good thinking!' said Zeno.

And, very slowly, they all backed out, down the marble steps, through the fortified doors and the electric gates, then hurried into the night as fast as they could go.

Shylo was the last to leave. Suddenly, he was no

longer so afraid of the weeping tiger. In fact, he felt sorry for her and his compassion melted his fear. She seemed to have deflated like a balloon and was now shrivelled and damp.

He took one last look at the empty display case - just to check that the diamond really wasn't there - and, as he did so, his highly sensitive nose caught a whiff of the most delicious scent. It wasn't Amura's sickly-sweet smell, nor was it the smell of Ratzi, mink or wolf. It was something else . . . something familiar perhaps . . . But then Amura started to roar again and Shylo turned and hurried out of the mansion, all the way on to the rolling grass of Hampstead Heath. Even then he could still hear the tigress's howl echoing across the hills:

'MY BEAUTIFUL DIAMOND! WHO HAS STOLEN MY BEAUTIFUL DIAMOND? I WANT MY DIAMOND *NOOOOWWWW!*'

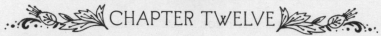 CHAPTER TWELVE

'Baffling!' said Nelson when the Royal Rabbits returned from their expedition.

Clooney flopped on to the sofa of the war room and undid his bow tie. Laser fell into an armchair, and Zeno, who couldn't sit down because of falling on his behind so many times during his judo lesson, positioned himself beside Nelson's desk with his muscly arms folded.

Horatio, who was in the other armchair with his stump on a stool, closed the book he had been reading and looked at Shylo expectantly. 'Why don't you tell us exactly what happened when you went inside, Shylo?' he asked.

Shylo stood in the middle of the room. He was very nervous because everyone was staring at him again, but he summoned his courage and began to tell his tale from the moment he had entered Tiger Towers. He made sure not to miss out a single detail (he even told them about the marshmallow and caviar and how sick he had felt) because he hoped there might be something in his story that gave away the identity of the thief.

'Extraordinary!' exclaimed Horatio, once the tale was finished. 'If the minks don't have it, and we don't have it and Amura doesn't have it . . . who does?'

They all looked at one another in bewilderment.

Then Belle de Paw flounced into the room in a sparkly red dress. 'Why the sad faces?' she asked.

'Because we failed, Belle,' Clooney replied from the sofa.

'Horatio was right,' said Nelson, shaking his grey head regretfully. 'It was a trap.'

'But Minsky and I chose not to fall into it!' boomed Zeno. 'There was no fighting, just a judo lesson. Then Amura screamed and we followed the tundra wolves into the mansion to find the diamond was gone!' He punched a fist into the palm of his paw. 'And we have no idea who took it.'

'We don't even have a lead,' Laser said. 'If you have any bright ideas, Belle, let us know. We're stumped!'

'*Oh là là*! Amura didn't have it?' trilled Belle de Paw gleefully.

'Amura had it, but someone took it,' Laser corrected.

'*Oh là là*!' Belle de Paw repeated and there was something in the jolly way she sang it that put a niggle into Shylo's belly. 'We have to find out who stole it,'

Belle de Paw continued much too cheerfully. 'It must be a very clever animal to steal it right from under the noses of all of you. In fact, I cannot imagine what kind of animal has that level of intelligence to outwit Royal Rabbits, Mink-Bosses and tundra wolves!'

'And a very scary tiger,' Shylo added, watching Belle de Paw carefully.

'Amura must be very upset to have lost the diamond,' Belle de Paw said with a sniff. '*C'est la vie* . . . But I shall leave you to your dilemma – you clearly don't need *me* to help you work it out. I'm only good for looking into the periscopes. Shame! I will do as the Generalissimo ordered and see what is happening in the palace.'

She flounced off to the periscopes, which were lined up in a row at one end of the war room, giving her a view of every room in the palace.

At that moment, Shylo felt another twitch inside his

belly. A niggle. This time he thought he knew *exactly* why it was niggling, but there was only one way to find out for sure . . .

Nelson sighed. He had not noticed Belle de Paw's seething fury. 'I suppose we had better inform ST-BT. Clooney and Shylo, go to Downing Street and tell him what's happened and see if he and his Backstreet Brushes have any ideas.'

'Actually, I'm still feeling a little unwell after the marshmallow and caviar,' said Shylo quickly, putting a paw on his belly that didn't feel sick at all, just anxious. He needed to speak to Belle de Paw urgently. 'Would it be all right if I went to my room? I don't think ST-BT would appreciate an accident in the Fox Club . . .'

'Of course,' said Nelson, who understood at once. 'Go and lie down. I'll send Belle de Paw to check on you later.'

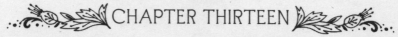 CHAPTER THIRTEEN

Once Shylo was lying down in his room, the door opened and in came Belle de Paw with a glass of ginger tea to make him feel better.

He smiled at her and she sat on the edge of his bed. Shylo's nose twitched as he breathed in her familiar scent.

'How was your afternoon, Belle?' he asked.

'Oh, I just took a little siesta and then sat in my boudoir and looked at my trinkets, and slept some more, and then you all came back . . .'

'. . . without the Siberian Diamond.'

'Well, it's not so easy to find such a jewel,' she said casually. 'Maybe we'll never find it. Maybe it's already in Russia. We should all forget about it now, don't you think?'

Shylo felt a heaviness fall upon his heart, for he knew that his suspicions were right. Belle de Paw wouldn't suddenly be so uninterested in the diamond unless she knew what had happened to it. He wished she would just be honest and tell him the truth. He couldn't understand why the Royal Rabbit he admired most was being so deceitful.

'Have you ever smelled a tiger, Belle?' he asked.

'I don't think so,' she replied. 'Why?'

'Because tigers have a very particular scent, and, when I was at Tiger Towers, tiger wasn't the only creature my nose sniffed out.'

'*Non?*'

Shylo shook his head sadly. 'No.'

'What else did you smell then?' she asked.

'It was *your* perfume, Belle.'

Belle de Paw shuffled uneasily on the bed. 'Perhaps *la tigresse* and I share the same perfume,' she suggested with a shrug. 'In which case, she has very good taste.'

'No, Belle. I think you were there.'

'How could that be? Don't talk such rubbish, Shylo!' She waved her paw at him stroppily.

'You said you wanted to come with us.'

'*Mais oui*, but I was told I could not! I should have been Nelson's first choice; no one knows more about diamonds than me. And, you know, I don't just like them because they sparkle, I like them because they are extraordinary.' She fixed him with her intelligent coffee-coloured eyes and Shylo knew there was much more to this clever rabbit than a love of sparkling jewels.

'Do you know that diamonds are older than the first plants? That a magical process occurs deep in the earth, a combination of pressure and heat, which creates these beautiful gems? They are not just lovely to look at but examples of what the earth is capable of creating. I like them because they are extraordinary and remind me to always be extraordinary too.' She folded her arms and lowered her eyes. 'But, even though I was the right rabbit for the job, Nelson ordered me to stay in The Grand Burrow and keep an eye on the palace. He dismissed me.'

Shylo felt sorry for his friend. He too believed Nelson was wrong in not allowing her to go with the other Hopsters. 'But you didn't stay and keep an eye on the palace, did you?' he murred. 'When we were at Tiger Towers, Amura had an unexpected visit from her hairdresser. That was really you, wasn't it, Belle?'

The amber doe looked down at her paws and heaved a heavy sigh. Then her eyes met his. At last, she reached into her pocket. There it was: the Siberian Diamond. She gazed at it lovingly.

'*Oui*. You have found me out. I wanted to prove to Nelson that I am just as stealthy and clever as Laser, Zeno and Clooney. That he should have trusted me with the mission. So I followed you all to Tiger Towers. I suspected that Amura has her fur dyed white and then it was confirmed when I looked through her bins and found the packets of dye. I guessed she must have it dyed very regularly to stop the yellow showing, so, while the tundra wolves were distracted by everyone else, I rang the staff bell at the side of the mansion and pretended I was her hairdresser. The wolf didn't even come and check – she just buzzed me in.

'After that, it was simple. You appeared at just the right time and lured Amura out of her bedroom. It

only took a moment. *La tigresse* had not locked the display case. I grabbed the diamond and escaped out of a window in her dressing room. *Fait accompli!* Job done! I meant to give it to the Generalissimo, but he has not included me since you all returned from Tiger Towers, so I think I will keep it for a while. It's beautiful, *non?*'

Shylo gazed at the jewel. How much more beautiful it was in life than in photographs, he thought. It was the brightest, most sparkly thing he had ever seen, like a fallen star. His gaze was drawn into the very core of it, as if an invisible force was pulling it deep inside. He noticed small imperfections in the stone. Some were thin and feathery, others flat, shimmering planes, but as he moved his head they changed. Suddenly, he saw the wood back at home. He recognized the tall oak trees near the Warren and Farmer Ploughman's farmhouse nestled in the valley. His heart was seized by an unbearable longing. He tore his eyes away. Up until this moment, he hadn't realized how homesick he was.

'You see how beautiful it is,' Belle de Paw whispered. 'When you really look at it closely, it is hard to look away, *non*? Let's keep it a while. It will be our secret.'

Shylo didn't know what to say. His friend was smiling at him with such joy, such pleasure, such utter delight that for a second he felt bad for not sharing her happiness. But then something else took over. Something stronger: his loyalty to the Royal Rabbits and the King and Queen.

'You have to give it to Nelson right away,' he murred.

Belle de Paw's smile faded and her face darkened. 'Nelson does not deserve to have it back. He dismissed me as if I was only good for looking through periscopes. But I am better than that!'

'You can't keep it, Belle de Paw,' Shylo insisted.

The beautiful doe clutched the diamond to her chest. 'Shylo! I thought you were my friend!' she exclaimed.

'I *am* your friend,' he argued. 'But it belongs to the Queen and you have sworn to protect her.' They bowed their floppies at the mention of the Queen.

'She has so many diamonds,' Belle de Paw said and waved a paw dismissively.

'No, this is not just any diamond. This is the Siberian Diamond, the most valuable jewel in the world.'

Suddenly, Belle began to cry. 'You're not going to tell Nelson, are you? You wouldn't do that to a friend!'

'*You* have to tell Nelson,' Shylo said. 'It's the right thing to do.'

'But I will get into terrible trouble,' she retorted, holding the diamond even closer to her chest. 'I have no choice but to keep it. If Nelson finds out I disobeyed his orders and stole the diamond, he might even expel me from the Royal Rabbits of London.'

Shylo felt miserable. He thought the world of Belle de Paw. She had been so kind to him when he was new to The Grand Burrow and was one of his dearest friends. He did not want to repay her kindness by making her unhappy or, even worse, causing her to have to leave the Royal Rabbits, and yet he couldn't allow her to keep the diamond. It just wasn't right.

Belle de Paw looked at him sternly. 'You mustn't tell a soul, Shylo. Do you understand?'

Shylo stared at her with big, sad eyes.

'If you do, I will never be your friend again.'

Shylo sighed heavily as if an impossible weight had fallen on to his shoulders. He didn't know what to do.

'I will keep the diamond because I have earned it,' she murred. 'I would like to keep you as a friend too. It's your choice, Shylo.'

CHAPTER FOURTEEN

Shylo was very unhappy. He didn't want to betray Belle de Paw, and yet he had sworn an oath to protect the Royal Family. He was a member of the Order of the Royal Rabbits of London. A wearer of the Red Badge on his paw. He had even been given a medal for bravery for his previous adventures. There was no question in his mind that his loyalties lay with them. Yet he did not want to upset his friend. There had to be another way.

For two days, Shylo didn't eat. He had been scrawny

before, but now he was just skin and bone. The Hopsters believed he was sad because it was his fault the diamond was stolen in the first place, as he had not been vigilant enough on duty. Only Horatio had a niggle that there was something more, but, when the old buck asked him about it, Shylo simply shrugged and replied that he was fine.

At night, Shylo crept up the tunnel to sit beneath the Weeping Willow in Green Park where he had found Clooney when he had first come to London in search of the Royal Rabbits. It had only been a few weeks earlier, but now it suddenly seemed like an awfully long time ago.

He sat beneath the stars, thinking of home. Yes, he had been bullied by his brothers and sisters, but life had been simple there. He had dug up turnips and gone to visit Horatio in his burrow to hear stories of the Great Rabbit Empire. His days had been long and lazy, full of sunshine, bees and butterflies and his mother's parsnip soup . . . Oh, how he missed his mother! He wished with all his heart that he could run home and tell her about his troubles and feel her soft kisses on his forehead as she reassured him everything would be fine. If he ran away, he'd never have to betray Belle de Paw, or the Royal Rabbits. He could disappear as Horatio had done and live out his days in the peaceful countryside.

But deep down Shylo knew that would be cowardly.

And, if he had learned anything from his experience as a Royal Rabbit, it was that he *was* braver than he knew. He was sure that if he dug deep enough he would find his courage. But he couldn't do it alone. There was only one rabbit who could help him. The very rabbit who had given him the courage to come to London in the first place when all he had wanted to do was remain in the safety of his country home: Horatio.

Shylo found his old friend in the small bedroom
Nelson had given him, sitting in an armchair in his
pyjamas, reading a book. The little bunkin stood
in the doorway and thumped his hind paw as he
had always done in the forest when he had entered
Horatio's burrow. It was the polite thing to do.

'Come in, Shylo,' said Horatio, putting down his
book and looking at him over the rim of his spectacles.

'I need your help,' murred the little bunkin.

'Tell me all about it,' said Horatio, taking his stump
off the stool so that Shylo could sit down.

'I have a terrible problem and I don't know what to
do about it.'

'A problem shared is a problem halved,' said Horatio
wisely.

Shylo took a deep breath and told Horatio about Belle de Paw, the diamond and his dilemma. As everything came tumbling out, Shylo couldn't stop his bottom lip from wobbling and a fat tear trickled down his fur, balanced a moment on the end of his nose and then dropped on to his jacket with a *plop*. The old, wise buck listened carefully, his eyes full of kindness and compassion, until Shylo looked up at him helplessly and said, 'I don't know what to do.'

Horatio smiled sympathetically. 'I think you do,' he murred softly.

'Well, I know what I *should* do,' Shylo agreed, wiping his wet eye with the back of his paw.

'Sometimes one has to do the right thing even though it's not easy,' said Horatio. 'In protecting your friend, you are betraying *yourself* and all your colleagues who are good and honest. And I think you'll be doing Belle de Paw a service, Shylo. I don't think she wants to be dishonest. She's backed herself into a corner and doesn't know how to get out of it. You can help her. You're the only rabbit who can.'

He put a paw on the little bunkin's head and stroked him. 'You know the right thing to do, Shylo, because you can feel it in your heart. Don't ignore your heart. It's giving you good advice. It always will.'

Shylo sniffed and gave a sigh. 'I won't ignore my heart,' he said. 'But, in betraying my friend, it will break.'

'Hearts mend, Shylo,' Horatio told him. 'They always do.'

·CHAPTER FIFTEEN·

The following morning Shylo made his way to Nelson's war room. All was quiet. The rest of The Grand Burrow was enjoying a hearty breakfast in the hall, but Shylo knew he wouldn't be able to eat until he had done the terrible thing he had to do: inform Nelson that Belle de Paw had the diamond.

He shuffled slowly down the corridor, his hind paws heavy as if they were filled with mud. He knew he'd find the Generalissimo at his desk, because he was always there, working day and night, in his green uniform and military boots, spectacles on his nose, expression serious and full of concentration. Shylo wished there was some way that he could avoid it. But he couldn't. He had to do what was right. He had to be true to himself, just like Horatio had said.

Frisby was in her usual position by the double doors. Crimson jacket pressed, gold buttons shining, nose in the air, baton in paw, ready to knock.

'I need to see Nelson,' said Shylo, and Frisby, who was usually brisk and self-important, gave him a kind smile because the poor little bunny looked so sad.

She rapped three times on the door. 'Shylo,' she announced and she pushed it open. Shylo took a deep breath then hopped inside.

Nelson looked up from his desk. He registered Shylo's floppy ears and sagging shoulders and frowned. Then he took off his glasses and examined the bunkin more intensely. 'Good greengage, Shylo, you look as if you've come to tell me the palace has burned down! What on earth has happened?' Shylo hopped slowly towards his desk. The Generalissimo's face grew more concerned. 'What is it, Shylo? Out with it!'

'I have news about . . .' he murred in a voice so quiet it was almost a whisper.

'What? What news?'

Shylo took another deep breath, gave a little sniff and wiped his nose with the back of his paw.

Suddenly, the door opened. Belle de Paw strode in, followed by a very cross Frisby waving her baton in the air. 'You can't just walk in like this!' the Major-domo protested angrily.

Belle de Paw stood before Nelson. 'I have it,' she said, and she put a package wrapped in a shawl on Nelson's desk.

Shylo stared at Belle de Paw in amazement. When she gazed back at him, her eyes were full of sorrow and remorse. Shylo's heart melted like ice cream in sunshine. Hesitantly, he put out his paw. Belle de Paw looked at it, then she looked at Shylo as if surprised that he should forgive her so readily, and took it.

Nelson stood up. He stared down at the shawl. 'What is this?' he asked.

'Open it,' said Belle de Paw.

Nelson frowned at her. 'It can't be!'

'It is,' she murred softly. 'It's what you've been looking for.'

The Generalissimo unwrapped the shawl, and there, sparkling and twinkling and glittering, was the famous Siberian Diamond.

Nelson gasped.

He put out his paw and touched it. Then he raised his eyes to the two rabbits standing before him. 'How did you get it?'

Belle de Paw looked uncomfortable. She shuffled

and bit her bottom lip. Her big brown eyes shone.

Shylo cut in, desperate to save his friend from getting into trouble. 'Well, you see—'

'No, Shylo,' interrupted Belle de Paw. 'I think it's time to tell the truth. Telling the truth is always the right thing to do.'

And so she told Nelson her story, from the beginning. Nelson listened to every word without taking his eyes off her and said nothing. Shylo wondered what the Generalissimo would do. He feared Nelson would be angry and would punish Belle. Maybe he would banish her from The Grand Burrow, rub out her Red Badge and strip her of the Order of the Royal Rabbits of London as Belle had feared. Perhaps he'd send her into exile in the countryside, or even back to France.

But the Generalissimo didn't do any of those things because Nelson was nothing if not wise. 'Why did you do it, Belle de Paw?' he asked.

'To prove to you that I could.'

He nodded thoughtfully. 'I see,' he growled.

Belle de Paw hung her head in shame. 'I'm sorry, Generalissimo,' she murred. 'I was angry because I felt overlooked, so I stole the diamond to prove I was as brave and cunning as the others. But I was only thinking of myself and my hurt pride. It is my duty to serve the Royal Family and to take my orders from you. I was wrong and I am sorry for it. I deserve whatever price you ask me to pay.'

Nelson rubbed his chin pensively. Then he shifted his eyes from Belle de Paw to Shylo. 'And *you* knew about this and were coming to tell me, Shylo?' he said. Shylo nodded and Belle de Paw squeezed his paw to reassure him that she understood why he had come to tell Nelson and that she was not angry with him.

'I imagine you have learned a great deal about

friendship and loyalty,' said Nelson gruffly.

Shylo nodded. He had also learned a great deal about himself.

Nelson turned to Belle de Paw. 'You are right. You were indeed blinded by pride and nearly broke your oath and betrayed your honour. But you didn't. The difference between an ordinary rabbit and a Royal Rabbit is that we will always do the right thing in the end. Good always wins over evil; greed always gives way to generosity and pride always yields to forgiveness if your heart is in the right place. We all have the choice to be better, to be the best rabbits we can be. You have shown courage today, both of you, and have been true to yourselves and your own honourable hearts.

'The diamond has been returned, which is the most important thing, and I do not feel the need to punish you, Belle de Paw. You have learned an important lesson all on your own. In fact, I admit that I have also learned something today. I underestimated you, Belle. I'm only sorry that you had to go to such lengths to show me. In future, you shall go out into the field with the others. I know you will be an asset.'

Belle de Paw smiled happily. 'Thank you, Generalissimo,' she murred.

'However, I ask only one more thing of both of you.' Nelson's gaze settled on them with all its weight, wisdom and kindness, and the two rabbits were ready to do whatever he asked.

'I want *you* to take the diamond back to the Queen.'

CHAPTER SIXTEEN

Belle de Paw put on a black yoga outfit which she had bought, intending to do some exercise, but had never worn. Shylo wore his usual red jacket, but he carried a very special cargo in his rucksack: the Siberian Diamond.

Escorted by a squad of four Thumpers, they hopped down the corridor towards the dumb waiter, which was an old lift once used for taking food up from the palace kitchen to the dining room. They jumped in and the Thumpers pulled on the ropes. Up they went.

Up, up, up into the palace.

'This is the first time we've been on a mission together,' said Belle de Paw excitedly. 'I cannot think of a finer partner,' she added, then she gazed at him with tender eyes. 'I meant to say this before. Thank you, Shylo. It's because of you that I realized I couldn't keep the diamond. Thank you for making me the best rabbit I can be.'

He smiled shyly, and she smiled back. A smile that held within it affection, happiness and trust. 'We all need reminding sometimes,' he murred.

'Indeed, we do.' Belle de Paw sighed. 'I shall be sad to give the diamond away, but it's the right thing to do. I know that.' She grinned mischievously. 'But perhaps I can look at it one more time.'

She put out her paw and Shylo patted it away playfully. 'Not until we're in the Queen's bedchamber,' he murred, bowing his ears. 'And only for a moment.'

They arrived in the old kitchen and hopped out on to the tiled floor. They opened the two-door hatch in the wall and snuck through, into the palace. The crimson carpets and gold-backed chairs, high ceilings and papered walls filled with enormous paintings were familiar to Shylo now, as was the smell of corgi. Today it wasn't strong. He hoped that meant they were out for their morning walk.

As they hopped through the state rooms and down the corridors, Shylo no longer looked about him in awe at the scale of the rooms or the splendour of the fireplaces, mirrors, tall windows and elaborate curtains, for he had seen them many times before.

They hurried on through the palace until they reached the Queen's private apartments and Shylo's sense of wonder returned. He would never get over being in the Queen's own sitting room and boudoir. He would never grow complacent about being close to

Her Majesty. In those rare and wonderful moments, he was truly grateful to be a Royal Rabbit of London, protecting the King and Queen of England.

Shylo and Belle de Paw lolloped into the Queen's bedroom. It was empty. However, the four-poster bed was not made and there was a large basket of laundry on the carpet, as if the maid had had to leave in a hurry. Shylo took off his rucksack and put it on the floor. He opened it and lifted out the diamond. It was very big and heavy for such a small rabbit to hold. He placed it on the carpet where it caught the light streaming in through the nearby window and sparkled.

Belle de Paw gazed at it longingly. 'It is so beautiful,' she gushed.

Shylo remembered how, deep inside the diamond, he had seen a vision of the wood back at home on the farm, and his heart ached for his mother and his warm, familiar burrow. But he said nothing and watched Belle de Paw gaze at it lovingly.

'*Au revoir*, precious gem,' she murred.

Just then, the door opened. The rabbits spun round in alarm to see a pair of black shoes walking towards them. Without hesitating, they dived into the laundry basket, hiding beneath the sheets. When they peeped out, they saw that the feet belonged to a maid.

She didn't notice the diamond.

She went to the bed and set about stripping the pillows, humming happily to herself.

Just when Shylo and Belle de Paw were thinking of jumping out and hopping to safety, in trotted the Pack. Messalina came in first. She wagged her stumpy tail, pricked her triangular ears and stuck out her tongue, panting excitedly. Then she sensed something delicious in the laundry basket and her tail began to wag faster, like a little propeller.

The other dogs trotted over to see what had

captured her attention. They stuffed their snouts into the tangle of sheets. Shylo and Belle de Paw swiftly burrowed to the bottom of the basket as the dogs' noses prodded and poked, this way and that, smelling rabbit and trying desperately to find it. Shylo pressed himself against the bottom of the basket. After this whole adventure, it would be very unfortunate if he was now eaten by a dog at the palace!

A voice shooed them away and the basket was lifted off the ground. Belle de Paw and Shylo put their heads out to see Messalina and her Pack gazing up at them furiously. Shylo was so relieved to be out of their reach that he gave a little wave. Messalina growled.

Then she noticed the diamond on the floor.

She gave it a sniff.

Shylo's wave froze.

Belle de Paw stifled a cry.

The two rabbits watched in horror as the dog opened her mouth and lifted the diamond off the carpet, settling it between her teeth. She plonked her bottom down and gave Shylo and Belle de Paw a triumphant smile.

CHAPTER SEVENTEEN

Laser was at the back of the war room at the periscopes, watching the action in the Queen's boudoir, when Messalina picked up the diamond. 'Don't swallow it!' she cried in alarm. 'Don't swallow it!' The sound of panic in her voice alerted the other rabbits and the place fell silent.

Zeno strode over to where Laser was frantically moving from periscope to periscope. 'What's happened?' he asked.

'Messalina has the diamond in her mouth!' she

cried. 'Now she's trotting down the corridor.'

'How the devil did she get it in her mouth?' asked Clooney, pushing himself up from the sofa and joining Zeno. 'And where are Belle de Paw and Shylo?'

Nelson hobbled over, the frown deepening into his fur. 'Where is she now, Laser?' he asked.

Laser moved to the next periscope. 'She's passing the White Drawing Room. If you dare swallow the Siberian Diamond, you dumb mutt, I'll . . . !' She was about to say something very rude but stopped herself. Nelson was a rabbit who expected good manners at all times, even when talking about the Pack.

Horatio stood beside Nelson. The brothers looked at each other worriedly. 'If she swallows it, the diamond will be lost forever,' Nelson growled.

'That will be one expensive dog!' quipped Clooney. But no one laughed.

Laser switched periscopes. 'She's headed into the

Queen's private study.' She turned the periscope around. 'I can't tell whether or not she still has it in her mouth.'

The rabbits held their breath.

In the Queen's private study, Her Majesty sat at her desk, signing important documents. Beside her was Lady Araminta Fortescue, her lady-in-waiting, and Sir Marmaduke Scantum, her Private Secretary. They were all looking very serious as the Queen's fountain pen swept across the pages.

The Queen glanced up as Messalina trotted in. She paused her pen over the paper and watched her dog. Then she took off her glasses, put the lid on her pen and pushed out her chair.

'What have you got in your mouth?' she asked, leaning forward with her elbows on her knees.

Lady Araminta Fortescue stepped back to allow the dog to trot by (she knew her place!). Messalina lifted her chin and wagged her tail as she approached her mistress.

'Is it a bone? You get far too many treats in the kitchen, don't you?' said the Queen.

Messalina stuffed her nose into the Queen's hand and dropped her precious cargo.

'What is this?' The Queen stared down at the diamond twinkling in her palm.

Lady Araminta gasped.

Sir Marmaduke muttered, 'Good Lord!'

But the Queen just smiled, a smile that was full of relief and joy and a deep, deep gratitude. She stared into the diamond, into the silvery flaws and imperfections that meant so much to her. And she found herself there in the garden, pruning the roses and listening to the gentle hum of bees.

She looked down at her dog fondly. 'The Siberian Diamond! You clever girl! But where on earth did you find it?' Then she laughed, her eyes welling with tears, and patted her dog on the head. 'Did *you* steal it out of the cabinet? Well, I am surprised. A little dog like you! We're all going to have to be a lot more careful, aren't we?'

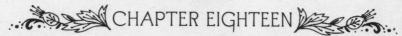# CHAPTER EIGHTEEN

Minsky-the-Terrible was in the *banya*, having a steam bath, when he read the news headline on his smartphone.

Siberian Diamond returned to the Queen – by a corgi!

How did that happen? he wondered. How did the dog find it? As far as he knew, there had been no corgis at Tiger Towers that night. But what did it matter?

He switched off his phone and sighed with pleasure. The steam was very pleasant. He was retired now; his days of being ferocious were over. If Russia wanted the diamond back, they would have to find someone else to do the job for them.

Then his gaze fell on the silver trophy sitting proudly on the steam-room shelf and he smiled contentedly. His team had won. But there was another competition coming up in Paris in the autumn. They had a lot of work to do. The French were not going to be as easy to beat as the English. He thought of Zeno and Laser, and laughed out loud. Those rabbits might be the most formidable fighters in England, but they hadn't a clue about judo!

Not too far away in Hampstead, Amura was lying in bed, making her way through a bucket of deliciously light and fluffy powder-pink marshmallows with caviar, when the report came on to her television screen.

'In what can only be described as a miracle,' said the newsreader, 'the Siberian Diamond has been returned to Buckingham Palace where it now sits in a high-security room in the museum. Buckingham Palace will not expand on their statement, which reads: "*The Siberian Diamond made a surprise appearance today in Buckingham Palace – in the mouth of one of Her Majesty's corgis. The Queen is delighted.*"'

Amura threw the bucket of pink marshmallows on to the carpet and yelled, 'SAPPHIRE, COME HERE AT ONCE! THE QUEEN HAS STOLEN MY DIAMOND!'

At the very top of the Shard, Mavis and Flintskin stood before the Doctor. The Doctor was very excited: it had been a while since Papa Ratzi had ordered a punishment. But these two Ratzis who stood before him now had let Papa Ratzi down and that could not be tolerated. (They had both determinedly blamed each other for the fact that rabbits *and* minks had turned up at Tiger Towers, so Papa Ratzi had decided to punish them both.) The Siberian Diamond was back in the palace museum and Russia and Great Britain were still friends. There would be no fury, no jealousy, no war. The Big Ratzi was furious!

Flintskin stood with his head bowed and his shoulders sagging, feeling very sorry for himself. Mavis, who didn't believe any of this was *her* fault, stood with her nose in the air and her arms folded over her flabby belly. Whatever Papa Ratzi chose to do, she would bear it bravely.

At last, the hologram of words rolled across the space right in front of them.

ONCE AGAIN YOU HAVE DISAPPOINTED ME! I EXPECT MORE FROM MY RATZIS. MUCH MORE!

The Doctor stepped forward. 'Here, Papa. I'm ready to carry out their punishment.' His narrow eyes gleamed and he grinned at Flintskin and Mavis.

Papa Ratzi continued to type.

I WILL NOT BE NEEDING YOUR SERVICES TODAY, DOCTOR.

The Doctor's face fell in disappointment.

I HAVE DECIDED TO SENTENCE FLINTSKIN AND MAVIS TO FIVE HOURS' TRAINING IN THE GYM!

Flintskin collapsed on to his knees and began to sob. 'Not the gym!' he wailed.

Mavis whacked him round the head. 'Shut up! Don't be so pathetic.'

Papa Ratzi continued:

AND A DIET OF CARROT AND CABBAGE FOR A WEEK.

Now Mavis sank to her knees and began to sob as well. 'Carrot and cabbage!' she cried. 'Take an ear. Or a slice of tail. But not carrot and cabbage - for a WEEK! I BEG YOU!'

YOU WILL NOT LET ME DOWN AGAIN BECAUSE I WILL CHOOSE ANOTHER MORE WORTHY RAT FOR MY NEXT PLAN.

Mavis stuck out her lower lip. Was this the end of her dreams of being famous? Of having her own reality TV show?

Of course not. She was not going to give up so easily. She'd think of something . . .

CHAPTER NINETEEN

It was a dark night full of stars. Shylo and Horatio had left the celebration party and crept outside to sit beneath the Weeping Willow. The odd taxi rumbled along the Mall, but otherwise it was quiet and peaceful in Green Park. The old buck and the young bunkin sat side by side on the grass, which was damp with dew and long beneath the tree where the tractor failed to mow. The air was thick with the scent of summer.

Shylo sighed wistfully, for whenever he snuck outside

in the night and looked up at the stars he wondered whether his mother was seeing the same stars and whether she was thinking of him as he was thinking of her.

His heart was full of happiness. Why then was it also full of longing?

'You did well, Shylo,' murred Horatio, looking at his young friend with tenderness. 'You had a difficult choice to make, between your friendship with Belle de Paw and your loyalty to the Royal Rabbits and the King and Queen, but you did the right thing. It all turned out well in the end.'

'Why is life hard, Horatio?' Shylo murmured, gazing up at the old buck, hoping for answers to the many questions that buzzed about his head like restless bees.

Horatio sighed and wondered how to answer in a way that the little rabbit would understand. 'The

only obstacle to success, Shylo, is fear,' he said. 'Fear that you're not good enough. Fear that you will lack courage. Fear that you will not do your best.'

He put his arm round the little rabbit's shoulders. 'It's all right to make mistakes, Shylo, as long as you learn from them. After all, everyone makes mistakes. You mustn't be so hard on yourself.'

Shylo knew he was referring to him falling asleep on duty.

'When you believe in yourself, you can move mountains.'

'But how do I believe in myself?' Shylo asked.

'One can always do much more than one thinks. When you were told to go into Tiger Towers on your own, you did it without hesitation, didn't you?' Shylo nodded. 'When you were talking to Amura, you somehow found the right things to say, didn't you?' Shylo nodded again. 'When the Pack tried to catch you, you ran away, didn't you?'

'Yes, I did.'

'That's because you didn't *think*, you just *did*. If you think too much, you let the fear in. You doubt yourself. You have to live in the now and not think about the future or the past. When you're in the now, you somehow find the right thing to do. Sometimes, Shylo, you just have to be brave.'

Shylo thought about that and realized Horatio was right. When faced with danger, he had found ways to cope. He really *was* much braver than he knew.

'If I could wave a magic wand and give you whatever your heart desired, what would it be?' Horatio asked, even though he was sure he already knew the answer.

Shylo looked down at his paws, because he felt a little foolish.

'You don't have to be shy with me,' Horatio said.

'I'd like to see my mother,' Shylo murred, and he

felt an ache in his chest where his heart was.

'And so you shall,' murred Horatio. 'I had a feeling you might be homesick, so I've been talking to Nelson and he agrees with me. It's time you went home and visited your family.'

Shylo's ears, which were flopping over his forehead, stiffened with excitement. 'Truly?' he exclaimed.

'Truly,' murred Horatio.

'Does she know?' Shylo asked, imagining his mother's face when he turned up in the mouth of the Burrow.

'It will be a surprise,' said Horatio. 'A wonderful surprise.'

'What will she think when she sees me?' Shylo wondered, embarrassed suddenly that he had said those words out loud.

'She'll be very proud,' Horatio told him. 'As am I.'

Shylo looked up at his old friend with shining eyes. 'Truly?' he said. He couldn't believe that, after the mistake he'd made, Horatio was still proud of him.

'*Very* proud, Shylo,' said Horatio, drawing him close. 'Very proud indeed.'

ACKNOWLEDGEMENTS

With our deepest thanks to Jane Griffiths, Kate Hindley, Jenny Richards, Jenny Glencross, Sheila Crowley, Luke Speed and Georgina Capel.

Hop over the
page for
some
Royal
Rabbits
extras!

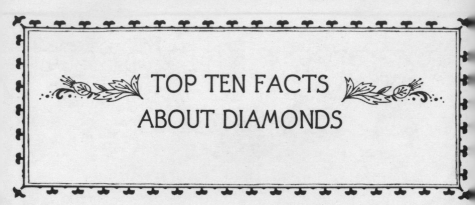

TOP TEN FACTS
ABOUT DIAMONDS

1. Diamonds are precious stones, which are formed when carbon is compressed tightly together and heated to extreme temperatures of over a thousand degrees Celsius.

2. Diamonds are found deep inside the Earth, from 140 to 190 kilometres down.

3. Sometimes diamonds will find their way to the Earth's surface through volcanic eruptions, but mostly people will have to dig or mine for them.

4. Diamonds are the hardest substances that occur in nature. They are valued as gemstones because of their beauty, and used in jewellery, especially for engagement rings.

5. Because they are so hard, diamonds are also used in drills and other tools to cut through many hard materials.

6. The very first diamond ever given in an engagement ring was in 1477, when Archduke Maximilian of Austria have his true love, Mary of Burgundy, a gold ring with the letter 'M' in diamonds.

7. The word 'diamond' comes from the Greek 'adamas', which means 'indestructible'.

8. Diamonds are measured in carats. The higher the carat the better the quality of diamond.

9. The largest diamond ever found is called the Cullinan diamond. It weighs a whopping 0.6kg, which is 3,106 carats.

10. The people of Ancient Greece and Rome believed that diamonds were the tears of the gods.

QUIZ:

Could you stop a thief

1. You're in the garden with your friends and you notice the back door is open when you're sure you shut it. Do you . . .

a) Shut it again and look around quickly for anything suspicious, then forget about it?

b) Assume it must have blown open in the wind and carry on playing?

c) Go and check inside to make sure no one got past you while you were distracted?

2. What is your ideal way to spend a weekend?

a) Reading detective books.

b) Playing at your best friend's house.

c) Spying on the neighbours from your bedroom window to make sure no one is up to anything they shouldn't be.

3. Your mum has made a delicious-looking chocolate cake but she says no one is allowed to touch it until after lunch. Do you . . .

a) Play in your room, but check regularly downstairs to make sure the cake is still there?

b) Wait until Mum's talking to one of the neighbour's outside, before helping yourself to a slice? She'll never know it was you!

c) Guard the kitchen door to stop anyone getting anywhere near the cake?

4. Your sister tells you about her secret plan to sneak out at midnight to meet her boyfriend. Do you . . .

a) Tell Mum and Dad? Serves her right for taking the last biscuit yesterday.

b) Let her go and keep the secret?

c) Set your alarm for just before midnight, then hide in the dark and jump out at her as she's creeping out?

5. Your friend tells you she thinks her brother is stealing from her secret sweet supply. Together you . . .

a) Hide the sweets to a better, more secret location.

b) Eat all the sweets so there is nothing left to steal.

c) Set your phones on 'video' mode and lie in wait to catch him in the act.

6. You get home to find that someone has moved all your things around and your room is suspiciously clean. Do you . . .

a) Write a large sign, which reads, 'DO NOT TOUCH MY STUFF' so this never happens again?

b) Ignore it - it's lovely to come home to a nice clean room?

c) Set up a trip wire across your bedroom doorway so that whoever comes in falls over it? You'll know who the sneaky intruder is when they tell you off about it!

Mostly As
You're pretty observant and good at spotting suspicious activity, but you're easily distracted – so be careful, one day a thief might just sneak past you!

Mostly Bs
You're lots of fun and you love playing tricks, but you're definitely not sharp-eyed enough to stop a thief!

Mostly Cs
Wow – you're super alert and inventive, and always on the look-out for anything out of the ordinary. No thief is getting past you!

HOW TO SPOT A MINK OF THE KREMLIN

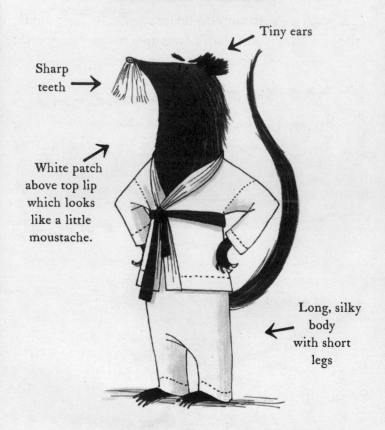

Tiny ears

Sharp teeth →

White patch above top lip which looks like a little moustache.

← Long, silky body with short legs

HOW TO GO UNDERCOVER

1. Carry a selection of accessories with you at all times – sunglasses, hat, newspaper, wig – so you can disguise yourself at a moment's notice.

2. Make sure you have a large bag with lots of pockets to carry all your gear inside.

3. Wear dark or plain clothes to help you blend in.

4. Carry a notebook to help you keep track of clues and solve cases.

5. Having a partner can make going undercover much more fun – team up with a friend or a brother or sister and work together!

6. Good luck!

HAVE YOU READ ALL OF
SHYLO'S ADVENTURES?

'*The Royal Rabbits* is sweet, funny and beautifully illustrated'
The Times

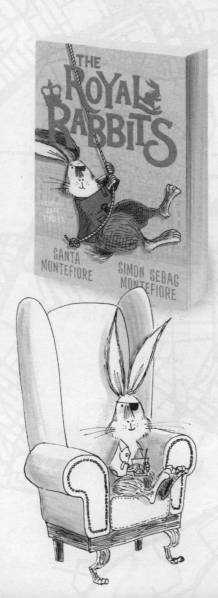

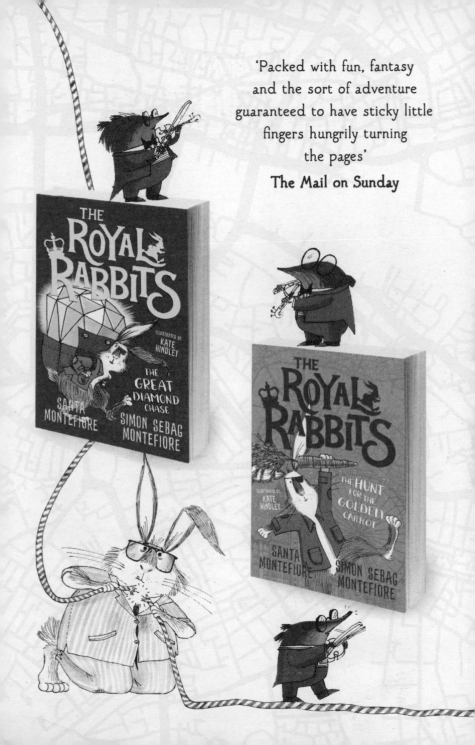

'Packed with fun, fantasy and the sort of adventure guaranteed to have sticky little fingers hungrily turning the pages'

The Mail on Sunday

THE ROYAL RABBITS

ILLUSTRATED BY KATE HINDLEY

THE GREAT DIAMOND CHASE

SANTA MONTEFIORE   SIMON SEBAG MONTEFIORE

THE ROYAL RABBITS

ILLUSTRATED BY KATE HINDLEY

THE HUNT FOR THE GOLDEN CARROT

SANTA MONTEFIORE   SIMON SEBAG MONTEFIORE